The Dark
Heart
Of the Raven

Or, *Even the Darkness*

Michael Piers

DEDICATION

To my imaginative and creative siblings: Noelle, Joshua, and Marie.
The core of this story began as our idea, not mine.

And to one who was a raven and is in nevermore
Although you never knew about this book, your presence is its guide.

Life is a deck that may be shuffled and reshuffled.
Sooner or later, it will return to the original order.

PROLOGUE: THE FOOL
MARCH 2008
Domanoviči, Bosnia and Herzegovina
90 miles SW of Sarajevo

I wished Kate were here. She would have pounded some sense into the others, figuratively and literally. I missed her, unbearably so. Her disarming smile, rough sense of humor, in-your-face attitude – everything about her was perfect. But now was not the time to think about her, and what could have been...

Hearing no response, I sighed, rolled my eyeballs, rolled over, and peered over the edge of the roof. Four feet below me, Willy Cunningham shot me a goofy grin and held up the hand that wasn't holding a hammer.

"Only this one. But I'm fresh out of the other kind."

Having asked whether another nail had broken, I sighed again. I'd known the sophomore for six months, and in that time Willy's maturity had not improved. Myself the only senior on the school trip to Bosnia, I had felt conspicuously old for the last five days in comparison to the kids around me, yet inconceivably young when I thought about the weight of history that these mountains and villages must bear.

"Think you could take over for me? I'm ready for a water break." Willy set his hammer on the porch railing, unsteadily enough that it promptly fell off, and walked over to the large orange jug perched on the plastic folding table a hundred feet away. I glared at him. Willy had never done a hard day's work in his life when we'd met the previous semester, and although he had since then learned some taste of trial and fear and the survival instinct, a true work ethic had not been among the lessons learned.

Willy and his attitude still sit with me like a mouthful of sand, however many years have passed since the two separate weeks in which I shared his company. We were in Bosnia to do work, not pound a few measly nails and guzzle water – if the contents of the jug were indeed just water, and the color of the fluid inside Willy's transparent plastic cup told me it was rather some kind of sports drink – but in the four full days that our team had been here it was far from clear the locals had benefited.

I *really* wished Kate were here.

It was time to get serious. We only had one more day before we returned to the coast and got ready to fly home out of Dubrovnik, and still the remote mountain orphanage didn't look much different than it had when our motley team of American high school students arrived to fix it up. Half of my time, at least, had been spent getting kids to stop bickering. The first day, it had taken more than two hours before a single sheet of drywall went up, and I may have been the only one from the party to notice the two Bosnian men taking it down later that evening. It hadn't been installed at all properly. It also didn't look like this was the first time these guys had undone the less-than-handy work of American kids.

I decided I'd skip the sports drink and reached for my own trusty canteen full of local tap water. The canteen had been with me everywhere I'd been for ten years, more than half my life, carrying in it the unfiltered water of four continents. Not once had I regretted a drink taken from it.

"You still surprise me when you do that" said a voice behind me. I turned.

"Why's that, Mr. Boval?"

"I remember you from last year's group. You seem like a smart enough kid to know not to drink tap water in places like this."

"Why, is it worse here than in Afghanistan?"

The coordinator of my school's annual visit to Bosnia went on like he hadn't heard.

"Drinking the water in the Dinaric Alps can do funny stuff to you. Lots of microbes in the soil and the snowmelt."

"Doesn't seem to hurt you. And I know you're not from here. You're Swiss."

"True, but I've been spending a lot of time in Bosnia since before it became independent. Been drinking water from this part of the world for a long time."

"Can't blame you. It's got a nice rich taste to it."

"Remind me your name. I'm terrible with names."

"Pedro Isaí Samuel Alvarez Gushvenbaych. Or just Pedro Alvarez. It's my third time here."

"That it is. I remember your face. So why are you here? And why have you come back this time?"

I frowned in some confusion. "You know why we're here, Mr. Boval. You have to because you organized our stay here."

"You could still try explaining it in your own words, though."

"I don't know. It's a mission trip. We come here, we help remodel an orphanage, we go home."

"Remodel an orphanage. Isn't that what you did last year?"

"Yeah."

"This same building, wasn't it?"

I looked away without replying. So it wasn't my imagination.

"Good job."

"I don't know what you're getting at, sir."

"That's not true, Pedro. I think you would have asked me the same question by this evening. Why are you and the others here?"

I looked beyond the ramshackle building to the hills around

it, still covered with the charred trunks of trees consumed by the wildfire of last summer. The vista had changed quite a bit since last year, far more than the construction site.

"We're definitely not here to build an orphanage. The locals are more than capable of building anything this town needs." I looked back at the building we were supposedly constructing. "It's not even an orphanage, is it? The kids running around all have homes to go back to, I bet."

Mr. Boval nodded slowly. I knew he was from Switzerland, a journalist by training, and had been in Sarajevo during the siege more than a decade ago. Whether he was about thirty years old or almost sixty, though, I couldn't guess.

"So what's it really for?" I asked.

"Pedro, you wouldn't happen to be Catholic, would you?"

"What does that have to do with this? Yeah, I mean I was brought up in the Church, I'm a confirmed member, I think my faith is a big part of my life…"

"So you know what Medugorje, a few miles that way, is famous for." He hadn't told us this any of the years I'd come on this trip. I doubted Willy knew, though I did.

I also noticed that Boval said "miles" instead of "kilometers". Force of habit when dealing with Americans, I guessed, wondering if I should explain to him that I had lived in countries on the metric system for as much time as in the States. I decided that didn't matter.

"It's a major Catholic pilgrimage center. Up there with Lourdes and Assisi and Santiago de Compostela."

"Now, isn't that a bit odd?"

"Because it's in a Muslim country?"

I immediately wondered if I had said the right thing. Whether Mr. Boval himself was Muslim had become a running debate among some of my teammates. Some of the kids on the trip had never heard of Islam before 9/11. They had been surprised to learn Bosnia's religious inclination, some having a hard time believing that "white" people could be Muslim and some actually expressing fear for their safety. I couldn't believe some of the things I'd heard from classmates during our briefing meeting a week ago, and desperately hoped Mr. Boval wouldn't think I was as ignorant as some of these kids. He didn't seem to, though he could have given me more credit.

"This is a country where national identity is *based* on being Muslim. To the west, you have the Croats. They're Catholic. This town is on the edge of their turf, you understand. To the east are the Serbs, Orthodox."

I knew that much. Boval was getting to the important part now, though.

"Even in this part of the country, so close to the Croatia-Bosnia border and with plenty of Croats living on this side of it, a lot of people around here have good reason to be afraid of Christians. You know what happened here when you were a little kid."

I definitely knew, but suspected Willy and the rest of the group had only some vague idea.

"Personally", continued Boval, "I've lived around here too long to care what religion someone belongs to on paper. But I care where their allegiance lies in their heart. Do you believe in peace?"

"I do. I've seen enough violence in my eighteen years to hope there's never another war anywhere in the world."

Boval didn't press for details.

"If only that were possible. Every new generation comes into a world that's just beginning to heal from the wounds of the last one. That's why you're here, young Mr. Alvarez. So that the kids of this town can see that people who are different from them don't have to be dangerous, like a lot of people who grew up during the war might think. The people in this neighborhood are Muslim. Almost everybody else in town is Catholic. It's like this in most of Bosnia, whether it's Croats or Serbs, Muslims here have to share their country with one kind of Christians or another. I think this generation will overcome that particular division…but in places like this where few tourists ever come, you have to wonder what picture young people get of the outside world. You're representing a whole way of life to anyone you meet here."

I looked at Willy and the others, screwing around.

"That's a frightening thought."

"Don't worry about it. It's a good thing for people to see what Americans are really like. Yeah, they're annoying as all hell sometimes, but groups like yours do two things for your hosts. One, a chance to practice hospitality and show patience. You'd be surprised what good it can do a person, psychologically, to have someone to help. Much better, in the long haul, than being helped. Even if it's real help."

As he said this, a board that two of the other teens from my group had spend nearly forty-five minutes nailing in place came partly undone and swung ninety degrees from its intended position. I had to laugh. So did Boval.

"Two, you spend money. This building? It was going to get demolished five years ago, but they figured they could use it as a pretext to get rich American kids here and make money off of them. So you see, you actually have done some good. The rest of you just don't know what kind."

"But enough about it. You seem different from the other times you were here. Worried about your future?"

I didn't answer for a little while. What Boval was saying about the real reason for bringing us here made sense; my classmates, both on the "mission" trip and at school in general, came from wealthy families for the most part. But now he was asking me questions I wasn't comfortable with asking myself. Did the scars from five months ago really show that clearly?

"Mr. Boval, can you keep a secret? I'm not supposed to tell anyone about what happened last fall."

Boval raised an eyebrow.

"Honestly, I'm surprised they let me come to Bosnia after all that. At first, I thought they'd never let me out of their sight again. They're afraid I'm a fool walking blindfolded toward a cliff."

Now both of Boval's eyebrows shot up.

"Did this involve caves, Pedro?"

A chill went down my spine. How in the world did he know?

"I do pay attention to the news, you understand. Especially when the school that sends kids to Međugorje every year gets in the news for the wrong reasons...I've been wondering all week if you were one of those kids. Would you care to tell me what really happened?"

"I don't know. Except for filling the others in after we got separated, I haven't told a soul. It's been nagging at me ever since, nipping at my heels like a wild dog. But something tells me I can trust you. You seem like the kind of person who understands things. Maybe the time has come to set down this burden."

1: MAGICIAN

OCTOBER 2007
Along Highway 119, West Virginia

A coal mine. Deep below the surface of the earth. Deep even for a mine. Brazen Bar, it is called; somehow I know it. The men have never gone this deep. Conversations, whether about baseball or their wives and girlfriends (may they never meet!) or whatever else coal miners talk about on their way to work, have ceased. There's a little ribbing toward some of the younger guys who look scared, but even the veterans seem awed by just how much rock lies between them and the surface.

Jackhammers grunt away and chunks of coal break off the walls. Dust fills the air. Everything looks normal. Then the lights go out. Nobody makes a sound. One light comes on. Darkness seems to be seeping out of a crack in the rock, as if it has hands and a mind of its own. It is grabbing the men and pulling them into a crack that grows ever wider. All is dark.

Lights come on. Not in a coal mine anymore, but a barn in the woods. As below the earth, so above it. Darkness is reaching tendrils toward the light of the barn. There are people inside. A hoedown or something. Music is playing, people are dancing, whiskey is being drunk. I am outside the barn, creeping toward the window. Do I not want to be seen? It is as if I am sneaking up on them. An animalistic snarl begins to rise from my throat. Yes, I am through the window. I am not alone. We pile through. The first scream comes before I break through the glass, but now there are many more. The lights go out, except for one that crashes to the floor and floods a narrow swatch of the room with light. A fiddle flies from its owner's hands and lands in the light patch with a loud crack. A string snaps at one end and waves back and forth in the light. Back and forth. Back and forth.

I open my eyes. It is not a violin string but a windshield wiper. Back and forth in the driving rain.

"I said, are you going to be ready? We need to switch at the next exit. Make sure you're awake."

I force myself to wake up. Shake off the grip of sleep. The call of the quiet dark truly seems to have fingers and a mind of its own. I wonder what my dreams mean. That I've been thinking a lot about West Virginia, certainly.

Miranda Stillman, at five years my senior the youngest teacher the school has ever sent as a chaperone on an overnight trip, pulls into the parking lot of a gas station. There is a decently big space inside, out of the rain, with two or three different places inside that sell hot food all under one roof. Just what I need right now. I'm hungry and tired. We all are.

"Alright, everyone, fifteen minutes. You going to be ready, Alvarez?"

"Never been readier."

I will be. A little warm food in my tummy, some time to stretch my legs, and **Pedro Isaí Samuel Alvarez Gushvenbaych** will be ready for the remaining hour and a half of their drive. The end of their journey; now, there lies the less palatable part. Driving eight hours in the rain when the journey should take under six isn't so bad; setting up tents in the rain because the school budget is loose enough to let us spend three nights in DC hotels but also tight enough that the plan to camp all of the nights in West Virginia cannot be altered for weather, now there's the part that sucks.

"This sucks" says a voice from the backseat. Which one of the twits is it this time, I wonder: Trent Jackson, the hooligan who somehow has a 3.9 GPA even though he uses study hall to sneak around the faculty parking lot and shoot up teachers' tires with a nail gun? Chase Creighton, his emo friend from the western end of the state who's living with the Jacksons this year and might not ever be able to go home again after all the stuff he did at school last year? Willy Cunningham, the weird kid who talks about cows all the time? Probably not Brandon Parsons, the bookworm, and it's too male to be September Janney, the sheltered girl who has never been camping in her life.

It's Chase, the kid who supposedly pees on parked cars like a dog and wears a leather collar to match. The one who graffitied his own church back home last year with the Anarchy symbol and has a tattoo of it on his chest. The one who I distinctly remember telling Mr. Kretschak to "fuck off" in the hallway about two weeks ago and still got to go on the trip. I know it's him because I can recognize Trent's voice chiming in.

I don't respond. The sliding doors of their minivan open and the five kids in the backseat climb out. Not the five *other* kids; I'm eighteen and nobody gets to call me a kid anymore. Miss Stillman hands me the keys to the van and dashes inside, pulling her thin jacket tight as the rain beats down. Chase is the last kid to climb out of the van. He doesn't shut the door behind him as he and Trent hurry after the others to the shelter of the rest stop. I push the fancy clicker that closes the doors and locks up.

Of course it doesn't work.

The other van pulls up a few spaces away. **Thomas Kretschak** is as tired and cranky as any of the kids, and unlike my second-year colleague, the thirty-three-year-old geology teacher doesn't have a relief driver. It's the sixth time I have led this trip, and while Miranda is an improvement in terms of competence and pleasantness over the previous faculty co-leaders – especially my brother – the weather is not so nice. It's better than the year we had break later than usual and got snowed on, but, man, last year was so nice out. Last year also didn't involve *her* brother.

"This weather sucks. Where are we?"

Danny Stillman again. A junior, Danny has been voted by his classmates "Most Likely to Win a Darwin Award" two years in a row. Only two weeks into this year, Danny managed to break Mr. Ward's favorite coffee mug while the English teacher was out of the room for three seconds. Or as Danny tells it, he and three buddies were horsing around, one of the other kids knocked the mug off the table, and he got blamed for it because he was the only one who didn't manage to get back in his seat quickly enough. Danny's version might actually be true. I can imagine this kid someday committing a bank robbery and getting locked inside a safe.

"Danny, what continent is Israel on?"

"Shut up."

The kid who's just been told off is my nephew. Ricky wouldn't have been able to go on the trip, because of his grades, if his dad weren't Mr. David Kretschak, calculus teacher and one of the most highly regarded teachers at Berghall Academy. But at least he knows geography, unlike the social studies teacher's little brother.

Some apples fall further than others, I muse to myself. Even though I teach at the same school as my elder brother, our parents will never accept me as much. Not married, I have never given them a grandchild – something they rarely fail to mention, even though the grandson of theirs I know best is not much to be proud of. The Stillmans, though. I can't imagine how two siblings, even if they are seven years apart in age, could turn out so different. She teaches social studies. He *might* pass the subject.

"No seriously, Danny, where's Israel?"

A female voice this time. Lily Greitang, the group's master artist. Another sixteen-year-old junior, she's the leader of the art club and seems to nearly always be either sketching or photographing something. I remember hearing about the time last month she got a detention for drawing a nine-by-twelve-inch portrait of my brother on graph paper in class instead of paying attention. Doesn't seem fair. It was a good likeness.

"I don't know, goddamn it!"

"You going to write him up for that?" asks my sophomore nephew, who gets a detention for swearing pretty much every week. I sigh. Danny changes the subject.

"I asked a serious question, Mr. Kretschak. Where are we? You're the magician who put this trip together."

My navigator, the only senior in the vehicle, answers. Kate

Bauer has both the map-reading instinct and the familiarity with West Virginia to lead this trip herself. If only she had done her paperwork to be allowed to drive the van like Pedro, then I wouldn't have to keep driving the rest of the way to the campground.

"Danny, we're northeast of Charleston now."

"I don't remember going through it."

"We didn't. The quickest route to DC goes north of it. We're at the rest area between Spencer and Glenville. We cross I-79, go south at Elkins, and get to the first campsite in about an hour forty-five if we don't stay too long here."

"Okay"

"Any other questions back there?"

"It's in Europe, right?"

Kate looks slightly confused, then figures out what Danny is asking. Even Ricky looks appalled.

2: HIGH PRIESTESS

The poor man was utterly bedraggled. His clothes were not only shabby and torn, but too big for his smaller-than-average frame. They didn't seem to be his. He'd been found in a ditch, and while word on the street insisted he was reeking of alcohol, the doctors had found no proof that he'd had a drop to drink. Something was clearly wrong with him, though. His eyes were bloodshot, his breath rapid, his mouth almost foaming, as though he'd caught rabies.

The police inspector felt a surge of pity as he'd never known in all his years on the job. He knew this man, by reputation if not in person, and could only imagine what suffering he had known in his forty troubled years. It was a journey that, if the doctors were right – and they usually were – would not last much longer. This made it all the more important to record the man's last words. A power that could fell him would surely strike again and again like the killers in one of his books.

"Date: October 7, 1849" he wrote on his notepad. "Victim appears extremely confused about where he is and how he got here. Was found four days ago, having last been seen in public on the twenty-seventh of September in Richmond. In four days, has not been coherent enough to explain his condition. Contrary to word on the street, alcohol and drugs do not seem to be a factor."

The sick man looked up at the inspector with a weary smile.

"Mr. ___, I'm Detective Seamus Gannasas with the Baltimore Police Department. I come from a long line of detectives and I expect that my descendants for many generations shall be inspectors as well. Do you mind if I ask you a few questions?"

The dark-haired, mousy man nodded, then shook his head. Yes, that was okay, and no, he didn't mind? Gannasas figured he'd give it a shot.

"It says here that you left your home in Richmond about ten days ago, planning to go to your cottage in New York City, but you never made it to New York. Can you tell me what happened?"

"The high priestess."

"I'm sorry, I don't understand."

"I went too far, into the dark heart of the raven!"

He was silent for a few seconds, but kept going before Gannasas could find the right thing to say.

"There's a whole world down there, in the darkness. A lost world. A new world order. It's matriarchal, like the old societies of the Near East before the Indo-Europeans came. Do you know that term? It's something they're starting to write about in the universities. I touched the darkness for years and years…that's where all my ideas come from, you see? No journey was ever deep enough. I had to go further, further, further…we went too far."

"Who's we?"

"Brazen Bar, Cran Ross, too greedily and too deep. A victim to the horrors we knew were down there."

"Mr. ____, please try to collect yourself. I can't understand you."

The man had been slumping backwards onto his cot, but now sat bolt upright.

"The high priestess! The dark heart of the raven, don't dare go down there, you hear me? Some darknesses need to be left unexplored. Why do people fear the dark? Because there's something down there! I've had a mystical vision…into the very heart of our world. We thought we knew how the world works…but we were so very wrong. The new world order will come. Reynolds…may the Lord have mercy on my poor soul."

He fell and closed his eyes. Edgar Allan Poe would speak no more. He had died before Gannasas could make sense of his words.

3: EMPRESS

Pedro is soaked by the time he and the occupants of the second van get into the rest area. Mr. Kretschak is at the back of the pack of kids under his command, looking like he's about to shout one last reminder of how little time they have but giving up as all of them but Kate dash to the fast food lines. Kate, Mr. Kretschak, and I notice that all of the boys and September are in line at the burger joint, leaving only Miss Stillman and Lily at the somewhat healthier-looking Italian place. This late in the evening, they're the only two options; the coffee shop chain is visibly closed just when it seems like people would want it the most.

"At least GrubMacker's has coffee too", Mr. Kretschak mutters as he gets in line at the burger joint behind the slowest-moving kid from his van. Ahead of him, Jarri Kugmann-Torjaki is belting out rap lyrics like usual; whether the oversized headphones on his head are actually producing sound is always a mystery, but the stocky Finnish-born junior who flipped over a table in the cafeteria on finals day last spring doesn't seem to need electronics to keep his mind firmly focused on inane "music."

Miranda Stillman and Lily Greitang both have their food before the line at GrubMacker's moves any further, so I walk right up to the till. Kate gets in line behind me, but I know better than to insult her by letting her go first. The girl behind the cash register clearly thinks I'm a clueless, sexist boy, but she doesn't know Kate. Two months older and an inch taller than me, Kathryn Agnes Bauer is no lady. She's a force of nature.

Kate gets the same pasta dish – with alfredo sauce rather than tomato-based – as I do, and we sit at the same table as Lily and Miss Stillman. Just then, Mr. Kretschak walks by, switching his choice of restaurant, muttering to himself.

"Fuck this", we hear him distinctly, "I swear they've got the same doofus cooking the food as running the cash register. 'Fast' food, yeah right."

"I would put scare quotes around the 'food' part, personally",

Lily says to her table-mates as we pretend not to have heard Mr. Kretschak's profanity. She twists a bunch of spaghetti around her fork. "Got nothing on my mom's, but at least this looks like real food."

She gestures with her head toward the larger table where Danny, Chase, Ricky, September, Trent, and Jarri, in that order, have sat or are sitting down, each with at least one burger made out of cows that never saw sunlight and mountains of freedom fries that *might* contain traces of actual potatoes.

"How can people eat crap like that?"

"Oh, are you a vegetarian?" asks Miss Stillman, just as Mr. Kretschak walks up and looks hesitant whether he should try to join our table – four-sided and already full – or pretend that sitting with the school recluse would make any difference. Brandon the bookworm sits at a table by himself with his copy of H.G. Wells' *The Invisible Man*. That's totally Brandon, we all know. The sophomore gets about one detention a week for reading non-curricular books in class. Neither Kate nor Lily nor I, nor Miss Stillman it appears, wants to spoil for the others the fun of watching the geology teacher's awkward decision-making. Willy, the only one who went for the chicken nuggets instead, is still at the counter squeezing a veritable deluge of ketchup on his fries.

"Vegetarian is an adjective", says Kate just as Lily explains that no, beef is a staple of her immigrant parents' home-cooked Indonesian cuisine – just as a condiment rather than a main dish. It's right then that a commotion breaks out at the next table as September jumps up, knocking a few fries onto the floor, and swats furiously at her chest, then at Danny. An ice cube tumbles out of the bottom of her shirt. The boys laugh. She glares at them, but sits back down.

Miranda sighs. "Yep, that's my brother. Thinks slipping an ice cube down a girl's cleavage is the same thing as flirting with her." "He also thinks Israel's in Europe", Kate adds helpfully, leading Miranda to display an eyeball-rolling talent that many students would be jealous of. There's just a bit of irony that she teaches geography.

"What does he see in her?" Lily mutters just loud enough for the three people at our table to hear. "Actually, why is she even on this trip? Or him? They deserve each other."

"That's funny you say that", adds **Miranda**, "because I heard him tell someone over the phone that he's really just here to hit on one of you. Or both."

With slightly more student loan debt to start paying back than my starting teacher salary gives me in a year, I've moved back home with my parents and little brother for the moment. It's a moment that's stretched, so far, into almost a year and a half. Not what I went to college for. Something tells me the problem is only going to get worse. I pity these kids and everyone up to about ten years younger than them.

Who the heck benefits from young people piling up this kind of debt, just to get jobs at all? I wonder almost every day if it was worth going to college. I wonder what world I'm preparing these students, people barely younger than me, for living in.

Some, though, have more preparing to do than others. Danny doesn't get how sound travels through the walls from his bedroom to mine. If only phone conversations were the worst of that.

"Seriously?" Kate is indignant. "That's what hitting on me looks like? Even if he's just using her for practice…ugh, that makes it worse. If you're going to flirt with me, you gotta do better than that."

From my vantage point, it appears that Pedro gets the distinct impression she's really talking to him. Yep, Pedro and I unconsciously agree, he can *definitely* do better than that.

"You not having a burger, Willy?" says Trent, far louder than necessary, as he bites into at least his second. Willy looks stunned.

"Come on, you know I don't eat Cows."

We can all hear the capital C. Willy is weird. He likes to talk about cows, and that's all there is to it.

Mr. Kretschak chose none of the available options and has taken a seat at an empty table. I look apologetically at the students at my table, as if to acknowledge that I should technically be sitting with my fellow teacher, but before I get up it looks to the untrained observer like my latest bite of pasta went down the wrong tube. One cough, and my inhaler is already in my hand; I've had a lot of practice. Kate registers a look of serious concern at the second-year teacher. These upperclassmen are better company than Thomas, most of the time. They're so much different from the little twits at the bigger table.

Earlier today, I asked Pedro if he's ever had a detention. Yes, from accumulated tardies. Once. Kate, though…I looked her up ahead of the trip, since I don't know her that well, and was surprised by what I found.

Most people are, thinks **Kate** whenever this gets brought up. I've been in the detention log remarkably often, and for striking reasons. Reasons I will never think are fair. It's not my fault I forget things in my backpack and pockets. Rumors that I'm some kind of wilderness survival nut are true.

Yes, I thru-hiked the Appalachian Trail when I was thirteen. Yes, I lived in Flagstaff for the first ten years of my life and made my first rim-to-rim climb of the Grand Canyon at age seven. Yes, I'm better prepared for leading a camping trip than Pedro, who's an Eagle Scout.

And yes, I live in a wilderness shelter in my parents' backyard on all but the coldest winter nights. They're so supportive that I haven't even had a bedroom inside for nearly two years, by choice. I light a campfire in the backyard nearly every evening, and there's not a thing the homeowners' association can do about it.

So why is it such a big deal at school that once in a while – okay, maybe six or seven times a month – I show up to school with a lighter in my pocket? I don't smoke, or set stuff on fire between classes.

Unlike Chase.

Now, the time in tenth grade that a hatchet fell out of my backpack in the hallway and the school had to go on lockdown, at least I can agree *that* detention was fair.

Yeah, whoops.

Jarri is presently regaling the group with death metal lyrics in his native Finnish. It's still an active question whether he means for other people to hear him, or just doesn't care. Chase pulls the oversized headphones off his fellow junior's head.

The school record holder for "classroom disruption" detentions, at least among current students, crankily shoves his empty tray in Chase's direction. Since his aim isn't so great, it flies straight into Trent's abdomen. Since the seventeen-year-old specimen of immaturity is taking a big swig of soft drink, he chokes. Chokes, that is, and claps a hand over his mouth forcefully enough that the soda comes out another tube. Not his nose, but his *ears*.

Miranda groans. "I can't believe we still have another hour and a half of this."

"More like six days. Or is it seven?" Pedro has lost track.

Glaring at Trent, Jarri puts his headphones back on. So far, no one has figured out what they're connected to. Nor has anyone ever seen Jarri not wearing a hoodie. He could be hiding anything.

Danny tries to broker peace. "Why do you wear headphones that big, dude? You know, over here, they make little earbuds…"

Jarri, still wearing the headphones, cuts him off. "They made them in my country first. I had a pair before any of you Americans knew they made them that small. Lost them in two days. I like my stuff big enough to keep a full hand on it and not have to look for it. Okay?" Not caring for a reply, he cranks the music way up.

Danny, September, and Ricky interpret that last sentence inappropriately and laugh. Chase's mood seems to darken, a grimace spreading across his pale face. I notice that he spends the rest of the meal looking just as sullen as Jarri and Brandon.

The rain has stopped as everyone finishes their food, so they head back outside. Taking the driver's seat, **Pedro** decides to pull into the gas station – a separate building from the food court facility, but sharing a parking lot. From what I can tell, Mr. Kretschak agrees that filling up now is a good idea. The only thing is, the kids in the backseat are squirrely enough when the vehicle is moving. While I'm at the pump, Miss Stillman looks ready to open her door even though she knows it's dangerous. She rolls down the window.

"Please hurry. They're all poking each other."

"Another twenty seconds."

My prediction holds true just in time for the other van to reach the tipping point. **Lily** is in the backseat between two boys who seem determined to stay nine years old forever. I am so ready for this day to be over.

"I'm not touching you", says Danny to Ricky, holding his finger an inch away from the cross-country runner's eyeball.

"I'm not touching you", replies Ricky, his finger half an inch closer to the eyeball of the kid who still gets in trouble once in a while for inexplicably wandering around campus when he's supposed to be in class.

"I'm not touching you", says Jarri to both of them, his hands out of his pockets and his mind out of its own little world.

"I'm not touching any of you", says Mr. Kretschak through the window.

"Well gosh, you'd *better* not be!" chime in the three boys in unison.

"This is so juvenile", I groan.

"Pull my finger", Ricky says to me, holding it out.

"That's it! Can we switch vans?"

As I blurt this out, I push what I think is the automatic open button for the sliding passenger door away from the gas pump; in the dark, it's really hard to tell.

But it's the open button for the side where Mr. Kretschak is pumping gas. The door isn't smart enough to back up when it hits an obstacle, and it moves a lot faster than his reaction time. The line feeding the gas pump is sheared through. The hose flops away, spewing gasoline all over the van, the pump, Mr. Kretschak, and the parking lot, in that order.

Kate is suddenly very glad she hasn't been absentmindedly playing with her lighter.

The gas station owner is in a different mood.

"Y'all are gunna hafta come insahd", he says, indicating both vans.

The thirteen travelers sheepishly gather inside the gas station, the four legal adults wondering what this is going to cost the school and the nine minors wondering how much less time they'll have at the campground.

"Y'all some kahnda school group?"

Thomas takes the lead. It's my trip, after all.

"We're from Berghall Academy in Covington, Kentucky. Our itinerary is a few days studying geology here in West Virginia and then seeing Washington DC for a few more days. Berghall is a reputable private school and I can assure you we'll be able to pay for the damage to your facility."

"Ah, it's only a hose. That kahnda thing happens more often than y'all might expect."

But they're not free to go, because Danny has picked up a souvenir trinket off a shelf – a snow globe being held by what looks like a wolfman.

Danny picking something up usually means it breaking. This is no exception.

The sound of shattering glass is replaced by the kind of silence in which you could hear a pin drop. Danny, unbelievably, tries to make it look like a different kid did it. He can't choose between Chase and Ricky.

"It wasn't me! I didn't do it!"

"Right", says his sister, "just like it wasn't you out splashing in puddles last month when you were supposed to be in Mrs. Gardner's class."

Nobody even mentions the time Danny yelled "I didn't do it!" when a teacher burst into the room calling for a kid named Max.

"You wahnna know wah that there snow globe had a critter like that holdin' it? Know wha' that kahnda critter is?"

Chase holds up the remains of the statuette, which isn't too badly damaged in and of itself.

"A wolfman. Or is it a werewolf?"

The gas station owner shakes his head. "This here is one of the invisible ghosts from the Brazen Bar mahn. It was over one hundred an' fiftih years ago the coal mahners dug greedily into the black pits of the hills east of here. They broke through a wall down in the depths, into a cavern where somethin' fierce was waitin' for them."

The group doesn't respond. Eleven people hear only a hillbilly tall tale. Kate looks like she's heard something like this before, and **Pedro** is suddenly paying attention once the name of the mine reaches my ears.

Where, oh where did I hear that name before?

"The mahners had stumbled into the deeps of Hell itself, and lahk smoke from a furnace, out came the demons. No one could see them, even in the brahtest fahrelaht. Lanterns failed to cast anything more than the faintest shadow. They struck without warnin', lurkin' in the gloomy woods and preyin' on anyone unlucka'nough to get in theah way. But on the third day from their release, folks fahnally figured out there was one way to see them."

Chase gives the gas station owner just enough credence to ask. "How? Through the sights of a rifle?"

"Nah' quaht. Lahn up two sheets of glass in a row an' look through them, an' suddenly the true form of the ghosts was revealed. Faces of wolves, retractable claws like a cat, but walkin' on their hahnd legs lahk people. Nahther beast nor man, but ghosts. Demons. Critters from the pit. Y'all ain't gonna be campin' out in their ole stompin' grounds, are ya?"

Thomas looks bemused. "We can't know unless you tell us where the old mine is."

He points on a map. From Thomas and Miranda's expressions, the group can tell he is pointing to exactly where they are going to camp.

"Don' worry about the pump, Ah'm sure y'all's school'll pay fer it. Y'all be careful now, ya hear?"

Kate is the one who speaks next. "What happened to the creatures? Obviously if they were still running around, people would have done something about it."

The owner strokes his chin. "Ah'm glad y'all asked. The creatures realized their game was up once people started walking around with pieces of glass in their hands, and retreated into their dahk hole. But on dahk nahts, especially when the moon disappears and when the veil betwin the worlds grows its thinnest, they would still come to the suhface and seek anyone wanderin' outta bounds. Other tahmes, folks who didn' believe the tales, or thought they were brave enough, went out seekin' the critters' lair. Lord have mercy on the poor soul who got caught down in their domain. Not too many years later, durin' the war, a battalion of soldiers camped out near the abandoned mahn. Sentries vanished in the naht. Taken without a sound. When the other sahd showed up to do battle, they got too close to the critters' main exit. Both armies fled and didn't do any fahtin' until they was more'n twenny mahles away."

Mr. Kretschak starts again thinking about the distance left to cover this evening, and takes charge. "Thank you, sir, now if we're free to go, we will take our leave. Long ways to go yet."

The gas station owner grins at him. "You sure got a purty mouth, you know that?"

Thomas does an about face and, looking almost shell-shocked, gestures for the group to roll out. "We are leaving. Right now."

As they climb into the vans, Thomas is loudly muttering. "He's just trying to impress us. Crock of shi…crap. Bunch of crap."

Buckling up in the passenger seat next to him, **Kate** isn't so sure. Impress? No, I think. He was trying to warn us.

But about what? Ghosts don't really exist, do they?

"Something you guys have to realize", Thomas comments as they pile into his van, "is how tall tales work. Some people have incredibly fertile imaginations. People who start telling a story that isn't true usually don't believe it themselves. What matters is that their audience gives the tale credence. You listen to someone spouting nonsense, you just encourage them. A ghost, or a bogeyman, or whatever, doesn't exist in real life or in the mind of the person telling about it – the monster exists in the mind of person who believes the story."

"With all due respect, Mr. Kretschak", I break in, "isn't there a grain of truth to most stories like this? There are true stories about feuding families and inbreeding here in West Virginia, and in Kentucky too. They get exaggerated and made into horror movies, but the base of the story is real. In the 1820s, there were these two families who settled in the area he pointed to on the map…"

"How do you know about this?" Mr. Kretschak seems less supportive than he usually is of students as he pulls back onto the highway.

I'm not fazed. "I did my research on West Virginia history once I decided to come on the trip. Anyway, there were two big extended families, the MacGregor clan from Scotland and the Royster family from England, who settled in the valley where we're going, back in the 1820s. They hated each other right from the time they started building their houses. Like in Huckleberry Finn, you know? Stealing each other's livestock, hunting deer on each other's lands, that kind of stuff.

"This particular story jumped out at me because of something in a newspaper from the late 1840s. Remember, this was still part of Virginia back then, so it got into the papers in Richmond. There was an expedition into a cave system that stretched underneath the Royster lands, a small group of people from Richmond, who never came out of the cave. The local sheriff found out that there were at least two smaller entrances to the caves on Royster land and the Roysters were using one of the upper chambers to hide stolen money and goods. They already had a reputation for being highwaymen back in Yorkshire where they came from, and it seems they were still doing it over here."

Mr. Kretschak looks deep in thought. "Okay, so some family of thieves back in the 1840s murdered a few cavers who stumbled upon their stolen loot. Doesn't mean there are invisible werewolf ghosts roaming around."

"Here's the part that gets crazy, though. The MacGregors were a really rough bunch, worse than the Roysters. Rumors in the nearby towns said they mated with their dogs."

Mr. Kretschak scoffs. I'm glad the boys in the back of the van are all tuned out of the conversation.

"The sheriff claimed that MacGregor men had actually bred with dogs and created a pack of half-human, half-dog creatures, sterile but alive, smarter than dogs and able to walk upright, unquestioningly obedient to their pack leader. The newspapers in Richmond picked up lurid stories of, and I quote, 'abominations dwelling in the deepest pits of western Virginia'. Once that got out, people stopped caring about the actual details of the crime and the trail went cold. The sheriff wrote a letter to the editor of Richmond's biggest paper saying he wished he'd never said anything about the MacGregors and their dogs, because it made it impossible to focus on the missing cavers.

"Anyway, I was just thinking about how this all might fit together. These caves never became a tourist attraction because law enforcement blocked them off as a crime scene, and ever since West Virginia became a state it's never had the resources to do a thorough investigation of the caves."

Mr. Kretschak smirks. "A tourist attraction. That's all that these tall tales are. They're the fertile soil that grows tourist income. Urban legends get people to come check out the place, hoping they're the first one to see the Loch Ness Monster or Bigfoot or the Mothman or the New Jersey Devil or the Lizard People or whatever else. People like that bozo at the gas station would like to see the area full of cheesy invisible werewolf-themed attractions 'cause it would make money. Can't blame them for trying, but don't give that nonsense a moment's thought."

This isn't the reaction I was hoping for. "So you don't think Nessie is real? Or Bigfoot? I swear I saw Bigfoot when I was nine. My parents saw him too. I'm totally going to go lead an expedition looking for Sasquatches someday."

Mr. Kretschak doesn't say anything for a while. When he does, it's disheartening. "You know, Bauer, here I was actually thinking you were smart."

I don't reply. Mr. Kretschak is known as one of the most supportive teachers at Berghall. I drift into an uneasy sleep, wondering if something bad has been going on in his life lately.

4: EMPEROR

"We've got a problem."

No one sitting around the boardroom table disagreed. There were six of them in all, all the people save one who knew the extent of the situation. All were ready to assign blame, none to take responsibility.

"If this gets out", the first speaker continued, "there will be hell to pay. We've been getting away with this for too long, and we got used to getting away with it. We let our guard down. This leak *must* be plugged or it'll be in all the newspapers. Again."

"So what do you propose we do? Arrest everyone? Not going to work."

"I disagree" broke in a third voice. "Silence the little brats before they talk. There are a lot of ways they can disappear."

Uncomfortable silence descended as everyone realized Flandell had said what no one else was willing to. Three other heads slowly nodded. Two other faces frowned.

"You're not seriously advocating we invoke Operation Ussher upon them."

Flandell leaned in and glared across the table at Ovenden. "That is precisely what I propose if it comes to it. The stakes are too high to let a few lives get in the way. Vrienstma would say the same."

Ovenden wasn't convinced. She glared back at Flandell, Ylonen joining her. "You go too far. That's only to be used in a dire emergency. Which this isn't."

Ylonen spoke before anyone else could counter. "This is a problem, not a disaster. They haven't actually reached the spot yet. All we have to do is prevent them from getting there. They don't understand what they're dealing with and if they stay in the dark…"

Flandell interrupted her. "That's where they stay. In the dark. No one goes in, no one comes out."

Ovenden objected. "The only cave-in we need is the one between the perps and the site!"

Remstine and Little tried to speak at the same time, but as either would have said the same thing, Remstine, the first speaker at the meeting, went ahead. "Flandell is right. There are too many hands and eyes and ears poking around in there to make sure we can seal the evidence off."

A smug smile crossed Flandell's face as she faced Ylonen and Ovenden. "You're too young, my dears, to understand the realities of government work. Everything done in Washington has a cost in human lives. I was idealistic like you once, but we won't be making any more mistakes here. Other departments make people disappear into deep black holes all the time. This is no different."

"These are American citizens!"

"One of them isn't."

"Oh, so that makes it okay?"

"Don't think of it that way. We're making this country safer if we act now to keep the site hidden."

Ovenden and Ylonen still looked sick at the thought of what they would soon be party to carrying out. "This is wrong", said Ovenden, "not what I signed up for at all."

Remstine shook her head at them. "Something you have to learn sooner or later. Heavy is the head that wears the crown."

Little, in his usual fashion, didn't wait for a response. "Enough with the ethics already. We need to plan the details. Keep this from getting any attention. No paper trail, no deviation from the plan. Everyone sticks to their assigned role, we keep this quiet."

Slowly, every head around the table nodded.

5: HIEROPHANT

They pull into the campground. **Jatri** doesn't remember seeing a sign for a state park or a private campground, but it doesn't really matter. We're only going to be here one night. Tomorrow will be a bunch of looking at rocks and cliffs, before we go to the next camping site further south. It's time to get the tents set up. There are a few families camping as we drive in, plus a couple making out in their camping chairs just down the road from us, so we're not completely alone at the campground. Given this company, I'm glad.

I love camping. We used to go all the time back in Finland. My parents, like so many other Finnish people, had a cabin on Lake Saimaa, away from all the noise and grit of Helsinki. We'd spend the entire summer up there some years, carefree and in love with life. The cabin itself was more for respectability and shelter from the rain than for full-time use – I'd always get one tent with my sister while our parents had another, in the forested yard where we also did most of the cooking and eating and card-playing and book-reading.

Those were the good times, before the drunk driver, before the crash, before my father and sister were dead and my mother confined to a wheelchair in her prison of grief. She couldn't raise a child now, she told me, much less a son, and it was time I went somewhere to live abroad for a while anyway. I imagined Sweden or Poland, or maybe even France or Switzerland or Britain. When I found that I was going to stay with an elderly couple in America, in some city called Cincinnati that I'd heard of in school but didn't know anything about, I was surprised but more than a little excited. I didn't know what to expect about life in America.

It's my third year here now. The Cutlers had been planning to host one student a year, but decided they'd keep me if my program and my visa allowed me to stay longer. They'd also been expecting a girl to show up at the airport, but instead they got me. Somehow it's worked out. I miss Finland, but there's not really anything to go back to anyway. I've immersed myself in the world of my old hobby, computer hacking, and keep learning which stuff is easier to pull off over here versus back home.

So it's refreshing to once again be out in the woods surrounded by trees, but bittersweet too. Nobody here knows what happened to my family. Someone – I think it was Trent – caught that I said my parents *had* a cabin on the lake, instead of *have*, but I told them my parents are divorced and no longer share anything. It's common enough in this country.

I'm sharing a tent these days, and DC hotel rooms later this week, with Trent and Chase. People think I'm just like them. If so, these guys are hiding a lot more pain than I know about.

Tents are up. The trees are all dripping rain off their leaves, so that we can't really tell if the sky itself is raining or not.

"This is no night for a fire, I fear", I say, walking up to Kate as she valiantly tries to light one.

She takes it the wrong way. I have to get used to people thinking I'm a mean, thuggish boy.

"What, you think I can't get a fire lit? You're going to do it yourself because you're a guy and can do guy stuff? Fuck you."

She runs off without waiting for a reply. I wonder what's got her in a bad mood. That wasn't what I meant at all.

I find some of the others gathering between the vans. Everyone's wearing a jacket and a sour expression. Kate's not there, obviously, nor either of the teachers. Lily has turned in for the night in the tent she'll be sharing with Kate and September. Brandon is in one of the vans reading a book with a flashlight, while Pedro is looking like he's not going to stay up much longer.

"What's the plan, guys?" I ask as I walk up.

"I think we should go prank some people", says Danny.

"Let's see if anyone has beer", suggests Trent.

Pedro steps away. "I wash my hands of this. Don't do anything stupid. If that's even possible." He heads off to the tent he'll be sharing with Willy and Brandon, muttering. The last thing we distinctly hear him say is "If you idiots get caught and hauled into court, I never even knew you."

No sooner has the zipper closed back up than Trent and Willy have yelled, "Party time!" **Brandon** can hear it from the other van. I'm not sure I'm going to sleep in a tent tonight. At least in here it's dry, though as dark as anywhere. I think I've heard vaguely that there are new cell phones coming out that have flashlights built into them. It's a good idea. Phones right now aren't bright enough to read by, usually, and they keep going dim after a little while. So an old-fashioned flashlight it is. I'm reading H.G. Wells' *The Invisible Man.*

Hoping the raucous cheer from between the two vans doesn't mean they're going to invade my sanctuary of silence, I look out the window in the other direction at the rainy landscape. My face leans slightly toward the window as my head slumps. I'm tired. Maybe it's time stop reading.

What the hell was that?

I jump out of my skin! My book and glasses fall to the seat next to me as I scramble away from the window, shocked and terrified by what I just saw outside.

Trent, Chase, Ricky, Danny, September, Willy, and Jarri hear the screams and open the door to the van Brandon is in.

"You alright, dude?", I ask. I wonder if Pedro or either of the teachers heard Brandon. Somehow I'm thinking not.

"What happened?"

Brandon is wide-eyed, frantic. He calms down enough to say something, but by this point other people have moved closer and I can't hear it.

"Is he alright?" I ask Chase as the others shrug and walk away from the door, leaving Brandon inside.

"I think so. He thinks he saw something standing outside the other side of the van."

"There's nothing over here now", says Ricky from across the vehicle. "Let's do something other than just standing around."

"Yeah, how about some of this?", I say, holding up a tin-foil pan of unpopped popcorn, meant to be cooked in a campfire. "We've got plenty left for tomorrow."

"Assuming we can get a fire lit then", adds Chase.

"They did", says Ricky, pointing.

We all look. There's a family four campsites away with a nice fire going, and a few sites in the other direction the couple in their twenties who were making out earlier have retired to their tent – leaving behind a fire that hasn't been put out. I grin.

As the hooligans run off, **Jarri** thinks about joining them but decides against it. The sensation of camping, the first time since before the crash, is bringing up all kinds of feelings I can't explain. I find a sturdy pine tree to sit under. The pine is a comforting anchor in the sea of emotions I'm swimming in. Back when my grandfather was alive – he died before the crash and never knew about it – he used to tell me about how in the old days, if a Finn ever killed a bear, the animal's spirit had to be appeased with lengthy funeral rites to convince it not to take revenge upon the hunter. This would end with the bear's skull being mounted upon the top of a pine tree so the spirit could find its way to the heavens. Pine trees are the axis of the cosmos, bridging the distance between one world and the next.

That's what I need right now – a bridge, or closure at least, between the country I've been kicking myself around in for more than two years and the one where my heart and soul still live. I sit still under the pine tree, tuning out the sounds of the distant chaos, tuning in to the (admittedly minimal) birdsong and the presence of a squirrel chattering away in the tree high above me. I kind of hope to see a herd of elk or even a bear wandering through the campground, some reminder of the spirit world I grew up drinking in tales of, but for all I know they're extinct here. In the old days, my people – and others in Siberia, my grandfather told me – would raise bears from infancy and venerate them their whole lives. The living bear might be trained to wear a white robe and walk on its hind legs around the sacred fire, a physical reminder for the shaman and the tribe of the great power of the spirit world.

The squirrel, though, seems to be the creature calling me out of the limitations of my body, away from the electronics and death metal that I've been frying my brain with, up into the world of branches and needles and bark. I inhale deeply. The scent of pine, beautiful and intoxicating, fills my spirit, and for a brief moment I'm able to imagine I'm at my parents' cabin on Lake Saimaa, away from tragedy and the mundane distractions that have been poisoning my mind. The air is fresh and clear. The waves lap gently on the shore…and just like that, the spell is broken and reality comes roaring back with a vengeance.

Trent and the others burst into our campsite, high-fiving and clapping each other on the back. Or lower. I've never understood why American male athletes, as homophobic as so many of them seem to be, like to spank each other's rear ends. Nor, apparently, does Chase. Ricky "low-fives" him and gets a punch in the face in return.

"What the fuck, dude?" Ricky is not amused. "We just had fun here! Why are you mad at me?"

"Fuck you!" yells Chase, storming off without further explanation. I try to talk to him as he heads to the tent, but he angrily snaps at me not to follow him. I shrug and turn around, back to the group.

"What was that about?"

"I have no idea! He frickin' hit me!"

Trent shakes his head sadly, knowingly. "Let it go. You don't know Chase. Pretend it didn't happen and let's have some more fun."

Danny pipes up. "Did you get their beer?"

Trent shakes his head again. "No. I was just joking."

"I wasn't!" September holds up her handbag, which clinks several times. "Got two six-packs in here! Better drink them fast before anyone finds out."

Ricky whistles. "Whoa. Imagine if my uncle caught us."

Trent tries not to. "Your dad would be worse."

Ricky isn't sure. "Maybe, maybe not. He gave up on me a long time ago."

This rubs me the wrong way. "Be glad he's still in your life."

"I'm not sure I would mind if he left."

"Careful what you wish for, dumbass."

September butts in. "Okay, boys, we gonna drink any of this stuff? Let's get in one of the vans. Anybody got a deck of cards?"

I have to know something first, though. "What did you guys do with that popcorn?"

They all laugh again. It's Ricky who answers.

"We left it in those people's campfires."

I have to laugh too. We clamber into the van – the one I was riding in today – and soon we've got a card game going on the table between the two middle seats. "Bullshit", or "Bluff" – the drinking version. In my country, we could do this legally.

"One three", says Trent, laying a card on the pile face-down.

"Two fours", says Danny as he puts down two cards.

"Two fives", adds September.

"Bull on the fives!" I've got three of them in my hand. We're only playing with one deck. September grimaces, picks up all of the cards in the pile, and chugs half a beer. She leans back against the wall of the van, takes a deep breath, and belches as loudly as any of the guys here can. All five-foot-four of her.

It's my turn. I grab a six and a jack and lay them on the empty tabletop. "Two sixes."

"One seven"

"One eight"

"Two nines"

"One ten"

"Three jacks"

I almost call September's bluff again, but I guess it's possible she actually has three jacks. She's picked up a bunch of cards a couple times in the dozen or so rounds we've been through. I've only had one jack. I let it slide. **Trent** has a moment of hesitation before deciding not to call bull either.

Jarri lays down a card. "One queen."

"One Cow." Willy, of course.

"Bull on the cow!" yells Ricky.

It takes a second for everybody to get it.

*****

She watches them from on high. Pathetic fools, what do they know about the world? How little they realize the danger they've put themselves in. Swinging from branch to branch, she is unseen as they amuse themselves with foolishness. The van below her shakes with raucous laughter. Now is the time to strike.

*****

Something lands on top of the van. **Trent** isn't sure if he heard it, but Jarri sure is. He looks at the ceiling. So does Ricky. September's too drunk to notice, Danny too dumb. Willy, as wide-eyed as Brandon was earlier, looks over to the other van. The rest of us follow his eyes. It's still there, Brandon still in it, reading his book with no signs of alarm.

"Probably a tree branch", I offer as an explanation, but Willy has a different one.

"Cow on the roof."

"How would a cow get on the roof, genius?"

"Sshhh!" Jarri pulls his finger across his lips as if zipping them. There's a bit of irony there. He's usually so loud at school, narrating his every move or singing, profoundly annoying unless he's in his own little world like right now. I'm not sure who looks more like Frodo playing with the ring – eyes rolled back in his head, staring upward at something that's not there – right now, him or Willy.

Then the moonroof opens. I didn't even realize the van had one. We all freeze, wondering if a Tyrannosaurus is going to stick its head in.

Ricky, September, Danny, and Willy all scream as a body covered in mud drops into the van, scattering cards everywhere. "Holy shit!", I yell, not believing what I'm seeing. It's as if we've stumbled from real life into a horror flick.

The body is a woman, I realize, lying face down with her head in September's lap and legs across mine. She's wearing loose-fitting cargo pants that look like army camouflage and a tighter, dark-colored shirt. I try to move her legs off of me, but there's not a lot of room in the van and she's pretty tall. Or was. Oh God. I can't believe there's somebody lying dead on top of me. This can't be happening.

Then the body moves.

Everyone screams again. September shoves her by the

shoulders, trying to get the muddy corpse off of her. But she's obviously not a corpse, because corpses can't stand up. Or talk.

"Maybe this'll scare the nonsense out of you?"

Of course it's Kate. Jumping through the moonroof covered in mud – geez, who else would do something like that?

"What is wrong with you?!"

Kate turns around and gives me a death-stare that the mud all over her face doesn't hide. "What is wrong with *you*? All of you! Do you know how late it is? The campground has a noise ordinance. You've been causing a disturbance, you made tons of noise in that family's campsite just as they were getting their kids to sleep, and *is that Cooller Lite?*"

September tries to hide the bottle she's almost done with, but it's too late. Kate glares at her.

Ricky is pale. "Don't tell my uncle!"

Kate turns her death stare on him as she rummages through the pile of unopened bottles on the floor by September's feet. "Good grief. All of this is the same thing. Couldn't you have at least snagged some decent beer?"

Ricky shows about as much respect for Kate as he would for a teacher other than his father: not much. "Who put you in charge?"

She ignores him. "Get this shit cleaned up and get rid of the beer. I don't even care if you chug it or give it back to those people over there. Please tell me you haven't been smoking weed in here."

I can answer that question. "Unfortunately, no. Now if Chase was here…"

Kate rolls her eyes. "I wish Pedro was here to back me up. You guys are a disgrace. Get to bed."

Covered in mud, Kate clambers out of the van and stalks off.

"Yes, Mom", I call back sarcastically as she leaves.

"I hope she's going to take a shower", says September, quite reasonably. They are, after all, sharing a tent.

"Me too. I want to watch."

"Shut up, Danny."

Danny pretends to cry. "You hurt my feelings."

Now everybody tells him to shut up.

We file out of the van and head to our respective tents. I hope Chase is alright. When he gets like this, I have to worry about my friend. My dad's friend's kid, really; I guess I'd met him a couple times before, but he's from Paducah and I'm a lifelong Cincinnatian. Bits and pieces about what's happened in the last couple years of his life have started to come out since he moved into my house in July, but I still don't get why his parents thought I'd be a good influence on him. I'm many things, but a good influence is not one of them.

Still, compared to Chase, I almost seem like a respectable kid. Even I've never graffitied a church.

Jarri's tenting with me and my temporary roommate; Ricky has to share with his uncle, who I hope won't smell the beer on him; I think he had two to himself. Willy climbs into the tent in which Pedro is sleeping. I can't tell if Brandon's still reading in the van, but I don't really care either. Whatever floats his boat.

That leaves Danny, looking as usual like a lost puppy.

"Wait, where are you sleeping?" I ask him.

He mumbles something.

"I didn't hear that."

"Me either", adds Ricky, who's clearly in no hurry to climb in next to his sleeping uncle.

"With my sister. She can't share a tent with a student who's not an immediate family member, so…"

"You're going to sleep with your sister? Wow", says Ricky, "welcome to West Virginia!"

I almost chime in, but don't. Danny looks like he doesn't get it, as usual. Ricky gives up, sighs, and climbs into his tent. Following Jarri, I climb into the tent to find Chase very much awake, pressed so hard against one of the far corners that he's going to drown if it rains during the night.

There's awkward silence as we get sleeping bags set up, Chase and I sleeping on opposite sides of the tent with our heads at the same end and Jarri lying between us at the opposite angle. Jarri seems unusually serious, like I've never seen him act before.

"I'm just glad we didn't get caught." He finally breaks the silence. "In my country, people our age can drink in private. I never got to with my friends because I've been here since I was 13, but I guess it's a bigger deal over here."

I'm not so sure. "Technically, yeah, but in a lot of places cops don't give a shit."

"Yeah", adds Chase, "cops don't give a shit about any of the right stuff."

"And what would that be, according to you?"

The guy who deliberately peed his pants in front of everybody in the school cafeteria back in Paducah last year as a protest against the quality of the food, and who may or may not have been the reason our school has already had drug-sniffing dogs come in three times this year, has an answer ready.

"They should worry more about catching rapists than kids who just want to have a good time. Smoke pot, you get arrested. Drink, you get arrested. Drive too fast, download music from the wrong site, drive across the wrong state line with a gun in your trunk...it's like 'ooh, a criminal! Get him!'...but if you're on the football team and you rape someone and ruin their life, then sure, go ahead, you're an athlete so you can do whatever you want!"

He's been getting louder and more upset-sounding as he goes on, until the last bit comes out as a whispered shout. Neither of us knows what to say. Jarri tries.

"Did that happen to someone at your old school?"

"Yeah. It did. I fucking hate athletes."

"Even Ricky?", I ask.

"Yeah, even him. You think he's a good guy? You think he's not going to turn into a rapist in college?"

"Okay, can we talk about something else?", asks Jarri.

We don't talk about anything at all for a little.

"Have you really got in trouble for driving across a state line with a gun in your trunk? I still don't understand why your country even has all these states."

"Yeah I have. I didn't even know it was in the car. Dad usually keeps his guns in his pickup."

"Wait a second. Since when do you even have a driver's license?" He's never been able to drive the whole time he's lived at my house. I have to be the driver every time we want to go somewhere.

"I don't."

Oh.

Finally clean, **Kate** slips into the tent with a drunk September and a half-asleep Lily. The mud was worth it. I like mud, even if I have to sleep covered in it, but somehow I doubt either of these girls would be comfortable. Sober September would probably be mad at me for getting mud on her capris, although drunk September is letting it go. What hungover September will be like tomorrow is anyone's guess. Skadi's axe, she's only sixteen. I'm going to have to keep an eye on her all week and make sure she doesn't get into serious trouble once we're in DC.

"What was all that about?" Lily asks as I settle into my sleeping bag. September saves me the need to answer.

"I'm drunk!"

I clap a hand over her mouth, sshhing her. "What would happen if Miss Stillman finds out? Or Mr. Kretschak? You have any idea what kind of trouble you'd get in?"

September just laughs and pulls my hand away. "I don't mind getting in trouble! Rather get in trouble for something real, for once."

That, I can agree with. She continues, her speech slurring.

"You know what I got detention for lasht week? Wrong color nail polish. Can't have green. It's againsht dresh code. Shame thing for having more than two earrings or any bracelets or...fuck, I don't even remember what elsh they've got me for. It's like they want to criminalizhe being a girl."

I personally don't even wear earrings, but I get what she's saying. Although Berghall Academy doesn't have uniforms, the dress code is about three sentences for boys and five times that long for girls. Most of it is lists of items and hairstyles we're not allowed to wear. No this. No that. No, no, no. Then they wonder why students are so sarcastic and negative all the time. Or why sexism continues to hold women back throughout our lives. I've only ever seen two or three boys get in trouble at school for breaking dress code. Some girl or other gets a dress-code detention almost every day. The reason I'm not one of them is that I never wear skirts; "skirt too short", the single most common offense that gets Berghall students in trouble, is one detention I'm never going to get. At my height, I'd get it all the freaking time if I wore skirts.

"I can understand, September, but can you please not go getting drunk again this week? We don't need that kind of trouble. At least save it for senior prank."

"That's another year and a half. I can't wait that long. I mean, prank is usually after my birthday. If I don't do something crazy before I turn eighteen, I'm going to snap."

"What do you mean it's after your birthday? I assumed your birthday was last month."

"Oh, because of my name? Nope, I was born in April. My sister was already named that. She didn't go to Berghall so you probably don't know her."

"I take it she has an April birthday too?"

"Nope. November."

Lily and I both can't help laughing.

Chase, Jarri, and Trent wonder what the girls are laughing about. There's no sound from any of the other tents. I wonder if that's a good thing or really bad.

"So…what's the deal with teachers in this country anyway? I feel like Mr. Kretschak and Miss Stillman don't really like their jobs."

I agree with Jarri. "I've never had a teacher who did. They hate us, they hate each other, they hate the principal…I don't know why anyone would want to be a teacher. Every one I've had since kindergarten was miserable or just yelled at us all the time. Or both."

"Chase," says Trent, "there's only one reason someone becomes a teacher. Power. You can see it in their eyes. They love being able to control other people who can't fight back. They think they're so far above us that they're practically gods. And all they did to get there was major in Education when they went to college. Some of them didn't even do that. They've done nothing to earn total control over us."

"It's not like that in Finland at all. My teachers back home all had advanced degrees. You have to, to be a teacher. They only want the best people who deserve authority. Know how that works? Kids actually respect them. I went to one of Helsinki's toughest schools and I never saw a kid mouth off to a teacher. They don't have cops barging in looking for drugs…ever. Is that normal over here?"

"I don't know about normal. Kids at my old school in Paducah got caught with drugs all the time, but they never brought in cops to search the building."

"I mean more broadly. Do the cops want kids to be afraid all the time? Do the teachers? I feel like Ricky's dad does for sure."

"Okay", I have to ask, "how does it work out, the way your country does things? I can't imagine a school where kids and teachers get along."

"It works great! I never used to have very much homework. Came here and it took me the whole first week of high school to figure out that the homework assignments were for a day instead of a week! The Cutlers thought I was lazy when I couldn't believe I had to do all that by tomorrow. That's not what it is. In Finland we work really hard, but nobody, not parents or teachers, thinks that homework is the only thing young people should be working at."

Trent and I are confused. "What else would there be?"

"You know, learning other languages for fun, building treehouses, playing sports…"

"I had a treehouse once", says Trent. "We even got to keep it up for a couple weeks before the homeowners' association made us take it down."

Jarri looks really confused. "What's that?"

We tell him.

"Good God. What is wrong with this country?"

Trent is offended. "Nothing's wrong with this country! Just some people who live here."

"I meant no offense."

I press him for details. "So they let you actually have free time? Even in high school?"

"Oh yeah."

"And kids don't just run around...well, you know, doing all the stuff that I do? Somebody told me last year I'm the reason kids have to be kept busy all the time."

"See, I think *that's* what's lazy. Adults who think they're supposed to plan every minute of our lives. I've heard people at school talk about their little siblings and how even little kids are always getting shuttled around from one activity to another. When they get to be our age, they've never learned to manage their own time. People in *my* country grow up learning responsibility, and our teachers don't have so much control over our lives so we don't end up resenting them."

Trent is still not happy about Jarri's jab against America. "If your country's so perfect, why'd you even come here?"

Jarri sighs. "I didn't really have a choice. It was only supposed to be one year, but then the Cutlers told my program that they liked me, and next thing I knew I was going to stay here until I turned eighteen. Now look at me. I used to be well-adjusted. Now I'm plugged into electronics all the time and wasting my life."

"Not right now, though."

"True."

Nobody speaks for a little while.

"Let's try to really enjoy tomorrow, okay?"

For the first time in forever, everyone agrees with me.

6: LOVERS

JUNE 2013
Sedona, Arizona

Sunset will cast her cloak over the rock formations, bathing them in deep red light that matches their color. For June in Arizona, it will be a pleasantly cool evening, not that anyone living in the small home overlooking the red rocks would care what the thermometer says, nor the date nor time of day. It will be evening, two weeks before Solstice, and it will be pleasant out.

The woman will sit outdoors, cross-legged, wondering how much longer she will be able to do it. Another month or so, probably, before the blessing of fertility for which she now prays her thanks forces her into other postures. The figures will sit before her. Five are hers and those of her ancestors; the other two will come from the wildly different lands of the other ancestors her child will also someday look back upon. They will stand silently gathered around the central candle pair and the stack of incense sticks balancing between them.

"Maiden, Mother, Crone", the woman will intone as she directs her gaze to the three distinctly female statuettes, "Warrior, Father, Sage", facing the visibly male images, and finally to the one looking more beast than either man or woman, "Stranger. Watch over me and the life I carry, this night and each night to come. I thank you for this gift of new life, and ask your blessings upon my family."

She'll light the first incense stick in the light of the white candle and softly inhale as the rich smell began to envelop her altar. Sitting upon a blanket of sky blue, upon which her seven figurines also stood, the mother-to-be will let the memories of her childhood wash over her as she focuses her gaze upon the Maiden figure. She has entered this world not far from here, in the same place where her daughter or son will also be born in the autumn to come, between Mabon and Samhain. She might smile as she recalls the lighthearted days of her girlhood, climbing pine trees and swimming in crystal-clear streams, romping happily through the high desert in search of critters to take home or draw in their natural habitat or just observe and contemplate. And the many days of hiking the beautiful trails, paths through conifer and oak and maple forests in different corners of the land. She will grin as she remembers the nights sleeping under the stars around her campfires, even in the city where everybody but her parents thought she was nuts.

Another incense stick, and now her attention will be on the Mother, the being of intermediate life whom her body now declares her to be. She will be twenty-four years old, younger than her mother had ever been during her life, an age when so many people have never met the person they might someday make a baby with. And here she will be, already about to be someone's mom. She laughs, despite the sanctity of the moment. "About to be", who could seriously think that? She already is someone's mom.

The man will watch as the woman continues to burn incense, meditating before each of her Gods and Goddesses. They will be his too, of course, though when he prays it will be before two of the statues she presently uses and two others she never touches. He'll watch as she transitions from the Warrior to the Father, and a chill will run down his back. Warrior, he will have been for her since they first knew their paths would come together, though she has always been braver than he and the only time he'd actually seen war had been enough to drive him to the pacifist path forever.

Father, though…how could this be? He will still not yet be twenty-four years old, his birthday coming near the impending Solstice. The war will now have been half his life ago. Will it never let go of him? Or the other time he's seen lives cut short, back when he first realized how much he needed her?

As the man stares at the sun slipping behind the mountains to the west, he'll reflect on what kind of father he will be for the child. He isn't ready, he thought, but who could ever be? He had practiced leadership, at least, dealing with kids far older than babies and not much younger than him. When they enter the brave new world of parenthood together in the autumn, they will have much to offer their child.

Now the smell of incense will be joined by another smell, one he'd first learned to rat out before he learned, more wisely, to embrace. Whether the mother of his unborn child should really be lighting up, though, he still won't be sure.

The man will put his hands gently upon the woman's shoulders and rub her aching back. As if some vestigial cat ancestor lies deep within her being, she will purr softly and sink backward into his arms, letting her legs stretch out straight before her. Leaning her head back until it was parallel with his, she will gaze into the dying red light to the west and take one more deep draft.

"You really shouldn't smoke that stuff", he'll tell her, no longer really believing the words that came so naturally back when he was the straight-and-narrow preppy kid with all the awards, all the extracurricular leadership positions. Heck, he was considered valedictorian material until that business senior year when it was more convenient to sweep him under the rug than confront the tough questions that he brought up just by walking into the room.

She will swat playfully at him, dangling the pipe in his face. "Oh please. It's going to be legal sooner or later."

"I meant in front of our child. Smoking during pregnancy is bad even if it's just tobacco."

"I know that! Geez, you don't have to tell me about that. I never used to smoke, you know."

"We really both fell off the wagon, didn't we?"

"And yet here we stand. Two young lovers facing the great unknown." She'll put her hands on her tummy. "How can someone so small change lives so completely? It's just amazing."

"We're not standing. We're sitting."

Kate will box Pedro's ears again. "Ever the literalist! If you were any more literal, you'd be those people who opened that museum at the end of junior year!"

Pedro will groan at the thought. He'll just be glad their school didn't start dragging kids on field trips there until after he and Kate were in college. But he'll be far gladder that even though they went to different colleges – him to Columbia, as if he needed another reminder what country his dad was from, and her to Northern Arizona and her birthplace – they still ended up together.

"You're going to have to give me a hand up", she'll tell him as she blows out the white and black candles representing the archetypal Goddess and God from which the seven deities circled round drew their essence. He will be all too happy to oblige, latching each of his hands around one of her forearms and pulling her into a standing, tight embrace.

Neither of them says a word as the twilight fades further. They will listen to each other's heartbeats and slow breathing as if nothing else could be more important.

Later on, the candles and statuettes will be back on the shelves inside the small cozy home, and a candle or two gleams from every wall in the total absence of electronic light. Kate and Pedro will have saved every cent they've earned since being married almost a year earlier atop the nearby rock formation called the Cathedral, until they could buy the place and make it theirs. Six rooms in all if you counted the full and half baths; one room for them, one for their child, one for cooking and the one they were in now, the walls edged with deep couches and towering bookshelves and the center lined with low tables in the Roman style. Ample space it will not have, or need; it will be home, and that means comfort.

Their child will be born more or less exactly nine months after they have taken possession of the home.

"Did the goddesses give you any ideas for a name?", Pedro will ask, entirely serious.

Kate will nuzzle against his shoulder as they recline on the futon. "Frigg had a suggestion I found interesting." And she repeats it to Pedro, gauging his reaction.

He'll flinch. "She really said that? I can't...no. We are not naming our child after..."

Kate pinches his lips shut. "It's how you honor someone who died. We have a few months to think about it."

"Yeah, but someone like that, really? What about after some of our grandparents? At least they were role models for our child to look up to."

"Other than my mom's dad, that is."

"Well, yeah." Nobody talks about Kate's maternal grandfather, ever. Not back then, and not now. Even if he didn't commit those murders, he wasn't a nice guy.

"I'm not sure how I feel after naming our child after a kid from our high school who got killed on fall break. But you know, there's a lot I'm not sure about. All the big medical establishment websites say it's bad to smoke weed while I'm pregnant, but around here all the elders think it's fine. I'm going to stop for a while after tonight, though. Cernunnos was telling me earlier that it's time to let go of some things so I can focus on what I really need to."

"We're going to get our butts kicked this fall, aren't we?"

"Speak for yourself. My tummy's getting kicked enough right now as it is."

"Are you serious? You haven't told me yet!"

"Well, now's the time!"

Pedro will lean his stubbled face against Kate's tummy to check for signs of activity from his child. Sure enough, his future son or daughter gives him a hearty kick to the face.

"Yeah, don't get used to doing that!", he jokes to the unborn child. Kate laughs. Whatever the hell happened six years before the baby's upcoming birth, right now all is well in their world.

7: CHARIOT
Monongahela National Forest, WV

Today was a good day, **Pedro** thinks as the group starts to set up the second campsite. We're not in a campground this time, but dispersed-camping off a dirt road up in the mountains south of Whitmer. Trees are everywhere, a mix of conifers and deciduous, the former stark and forbidding, the latter in full autumnal bloom. Hues of red and orange blend with the dark brown of tree trunks and the deep green of the pine trees and the gray tones of slick wet rocks.

Willy approaches me, a sheepish grin on his face. I hand him our tent, still in the bag. As we walk over to find a place to pitch it, he looks like he's dying to ask me something.

"Spit it out." After last night's antics, I'm not interested in playing guessing games.

"What was the kind of rock Mr. Kretschak wanted us to memorize today? I'm in his class, you know."

"Tuscarora quartzite. Need me to break that down in syllables?"

Willy looks affronted. "I was just asking! Holy Cow!"

I don't really know how he could have forgotten. Mr. Kretschak gave us a nice long lecture at Seneca Rocks this afternoon, but didn't give us *that* much to memorize. Or, I should say, didn't give the kids who are taking geology for this semester's science requirement too much to memorize. Jarri, September, Brandon, and Willy are, I think, the only ones who will have to regurgitate any of the material from this trip on a test; Brandon tells me the rest of the kids who are taking geology at our school will read a two-page assignment on Seneca Rocks that gives all of the information Mr. Kretschak presented in today's talk.

I hope Willy isn't aware of this, though, since he'll probably just try to borrow a packet from someone on Monday morning next week. The thought enrages me to the point that I can feel my frustration running away like an out-of-control chariot. As if reading information on a page could possibly make up for seeing the real thing! What's the bloody point of going on this trip, for someone like Willy?

"Um…um…", he keeps saying as we get the tent poles set.

I'm in no mood for this. My goodwill is rapidly eroding. "Willy, what else do you need me to explain?"

"Well…what else were we supposed to memorize?"

Despite how nice today was, I'm almost ready to stab a tent peg through his head.

"It's. Your. Fricking. Class. Take. Fricking. Charge. Of. Your. Life." I spit the words out one breath at a time without moving my teeth apart for an instant.

"What's going on here?" Kate arrives just in the nick of time, and doesn't need a word of explanation. "Willy. Seneca Rocks is a formation of Tuscarora quartzite. The rock dates from the Silurian period, 430 million years ago, and was originally sand along a beach. Today, Seneca Rocks is the only peak on the eastern seaboard of the USA that requires technical rock climbing to reach the summit. There are more possible climbing routes on the rocks than days in a year. During World War II, the Army used it as a training base for soldiers who were going to fight in Italy and needed to climb in the Apennines. That was literally *all* that he said."

Willy grins. "Okay, thanks. Can I have your notes so I can copy them?"

Now it's Kate's turn to develop a Jael complex. "What bloody notes? I'm not in your class!"

"What? How did you remember all that stuff without writing it down? I guess I can ask Brandon, he had a clipboard…"

"It was effortless. I used this really super-advanced computer that I've got. I never go anywhere without it."

"Really? Where is it?"

"Between my ears, fucktard!" Kate smacks the back of Willy's head the way Gibbs does to DiNozzo every other episode, and storms off leaving Willy to figure out what she means.

The tents are up, Miranda and some of the kids have a campfire going, and **Thomas** is ready to do a little exploring while it's still light out. By this time of year, night can come quickly, but it's only 4:30 and I would love to see what I can find out in the woods. A scenic view, an unheralded rock formation, a crumbling old building…the possibilities are endless.

"Alright gang, listen up." With a black and white checkered bandanna around my neck, I almost look like a gang leader, or might if I wasn't otherwise a walking catalog for an outdoor sporting goods company. The five tents are arranged in a circle; closest to me, on the right, is the small red tent I share with my fifteen-year-old nephew. Better him than his father. Twenty feet away, separated by a few small shrubs, is the blue and white thick-striped canvas tent shared by the hooligans Jarri, Chase, and Trent; after that, directly opposite the campfire ring from the two parked vans, the neon orange dome the three girls are sharing. No risk of getting mistaken for a deer in that tent. Miranda and her brother, respectively the one person I pity more than myself and the kid I wish I could pawn off on Ricky, occupy a smaller dome tent another thirty feet from the girls; she says it's sea foam green, I just call it green. The camo-patterned tent with the other three boys brings the tents into a circle that the vans sit forty feet outside of. It's the perfect time to get their attention. I can already see Ricky getting a football out.

Yep, that's my nephew. Sigh.

"Who's up for a little exploring? This is a place where there could be interesting stuff to find out in the woods. Anyone wants to go check it out, follow me and stick together. Sunset's at 7 and we need to all be back in camp before dark."

Kate is in, of course. I struggle to control my urge to assume she's hoping to find the Mothman or some other monster. Maybe I could give her more credit than I did yesterday during the last stretch of the drive. Pedro seems to be eying the group, sizing up who's going along and who's staying in camp with Miss Stillman. Danny, to his sister's visible relief, comes with me, although to my surprise so does Ricky. Trent and Chase elect to stay, although God only knows what they plan to do. Neither of them should be on this trip. I didn't start leading it in 2002 so I could end up babysitting hooligans.

Willy the weird kid looks at Kate and Pedro and decides to stay in camp, while Brandon the bookworm is immersed in some thick fantasy book that looks like it's about a musical chairs game involving thrones. Lily the artist is sketching something; I'm tempted to try get her to come along because who knows what material we might find for her, but whatever she's drawing here (a tree?) already has her attention. Jarri shrugs and joins the small group by me, as does September.

We set off toward the southeast of camp, heading slightly downhill at first and then slightly more uphill. There's no real trail, but I'm leading them along what looks like an old path. It's covered in the first layer of autumn leaves. At any point, I can look ahead and see at least fifty feet of open ground ahead of me without any trees growing on the path. We pass between a pair of hills without seeing anything out of the ordinary.

"This is so cool!"

September Janney, of all people. I don't know the junior that well, but she isn't doing well in my class so far and openly thinks learning the names of different kinds of rocks is boring as all hell. Is she seeing something I'm not?

"All these trees everywhere. It's so beautiful. It's like we're in some amazing movie…"

"…or we could just be out in the woods." Kate could be in a better mood.

"I just mean, it's totally different from anything in real life."

"This *is* real life."

Everyone can sense the tension. I'm hoping September's sense of wonder, her innate ability to see the beauty of nature that no indoors-only upbringing can wipe out, is starting to take root out here. That's just what I look for in these trips. If even one kid starts to see what they're missing out on living in an oversized house on a cul-de-sac, and kindles a lifelong desire to love nature, the trip has been a success. At least in my eyes. I wish my brother was easier to convince.

"It's different from *my* life, okay? Don't have to rain on my parade, Bauer! I've never been this far from home before. It's awesome! My fourth state! Of course I'm excited!"

Kate says nothing. She and Pedro share a bemused glance before shaking their heads. September, mercifully, catches none of it.

We press on, September following closely behind me at the front of the group and the two jaded seniors bringing up the rear. Danny and Ricky found a small stone in the path some ways back and have been kicking it along between them for a while. Jarri has the oversized headphones back on and is spasmodically jerking his head forward and backward with the beat, silently mouthing lyrics.

And then all of a sudden there it is. I see only a low-lying ridge of rock with ferns growing all over it, until my nephew kicks the stone soccer-style past me and September and over the edge. From the sound, it's gone down a long ways. We dash ahead, curious, and find ourselves staring into the open mouth of a cave, built into the side of the hill to the right of our impromptu path.

The entrance goes down at a steep angle into the earth. Everyone gathers around and peers into the opening. It's a primeval instinct. We can't help it. Even in broad daylight, the cave opening, five feet high and about three wide, sheds light on only a few feet of the long tunnel into the blackness.

I almost make some pronouncement, but can't. September has been silenced. Jarri has been silenced. Kate looks happier than

I've ever seen her. Even Danny and Ricky seem to appreciate what we've just stumbled across. The cave entrance is half hidden with brush from any angle, there are no traces of any signs or barricades or steps built into the rock – I'm not going to pretend for a moment that it's an undiscovered cave, not in a state forest where hundreds of people go backcountry camping every summer, but it's got to be a well-kept secret.

In the end, it is me that speaks first, not any of the kids. "Anybody got rope?" I mean it as a joke. And should have learned by now that one does not make such jokes around young Miss Bauer.

Kate immediately has her backpack out and is unzipping the larger compartment. "Rope, harnesses, check. The shoes we're wearing should work. I didn't have space for specific climbing shoes, but I was hoping there might be a chance to do some climbing at Seneca Rocks earlier."

Mr. Kretschak actually looks impressed. "You've done any climbing like that before?"

"All over the place", I reply, beaming. "Used to go every weekend in Arizona. Red River Gorge once we moved to Kentucky. Mount Olympus, even."

"Which one?"

"All three." Utah when I was eight, Washington State at ten, and Greece back in June this year. I don't mention climbing up to a monastery at Meteora like James Bond. People at school usually think I'm making it up or bragging.

"So, we gonna do this or what?"

The way I'm holding the rope makes people realize I'm actually serious. Jarri whistles. Danny's eyes are even wider than usual. Pedro looks like he's just swallowed a lemon. Mr. Kretschak starts stroking his beard and looking at the sky.

"This is a terrible idea", we can all hear him mutter. "No

permit, no idea what's inside…oh what the hell. Let's try it."

For the first time all trip, everyone gathered around has the same facial expression.

With me belaying and Pedro all too happy to hold onto my harness for extra grounding, Mr. Kretschak slowly steps into the cavern. The light of his headlamp shows that the ground is sloping enough for him to walk about eight feet in before he has to start putting his weight on the ropes. He climbs slowly down until his head is out of sight for anyone standing outside the cave. I don't have to tell him to stop.

"What do you see?", calls Pedro.

"Holy shit!" The pause that follows feels impossibly long.

"Are you okay?", I yell into the cave opening.

"I'm great! You won't believe what's down here."

We wait for him to elaborate. The rope suddenly starts to jerk. I dig my heels in as Pedro grabs my waist and Jarri the rope, suddenly feeling like this was a very bad idea. But the jerking stops. Mr. Kretschak's voice comes from a little lower down. He's just climbing further down, I realize…but something feels wrong. I can't put a finger on it.

Thomas looks around at the surprisingly big cavern beneath the initial narrow shaft. There's a lot more room down here than I had expected, but it's not just that. There are timber stairs along the wall to my left as I face the opening, about fifteen feet from where I dangle along the now-vertical wall. If I get enough slack, I think I can swing over to them. There's enough rope I can go about a hundred feet down from where I currently am.

I wonder how the stairs got there. Clearly someone came in a different way than I have. Looking down, I see that the floor is a long way below and has, at least, a few piles of man-made objects scattered around it. They're covered with some kind of canvas. I wonder if my rope can go down far enough to touch any of it. And then, just out of curiosity, I look straight up.

I yell "Holy shit!" again, but this time from shock. It looks like a gigantic human skull leering out of the darkness at me, though as I catch myself against the wall I realize it's a few folds in the roof of the cavern further into the hill than the entrance. Three or four different rock formations, all of them at different distances, that don't form the image as I sway back and forth or side to side. You have to be looking from this one angle to see the gigantic death's head looming in the cave ceiling.

"No, I'm okay!", I shout my reassurances to the kids above. "I think it's an old mine pit. There's some stairs further in. I can't quite reach them from here. Going to try swinging a bit more."

Outside, the kids can't really hear most of the words my uncle is saying, but **Ricky** gets the urge to see if there are other entrances to the cave. I don't want to even set foot into the entrance we've found, since the floor clearly starts to drop off and it wouldn't be safe to lean over the edge. I do want to see for myself what he's talking about. Wordlessly, I gesture to Danny and we head a little further along the unmarked trail. Around the bend, we start to head up the hill. There's a particular tuft of vegetation about fifty feet above where the other kids are standing that gets my interest.

Sure enough, it's another opening! We clear some vegetation and discover there's nothing underneath but open air. Barely a foot wide, this narrow shaft looks decidedly man-made. There are marks from a lot of times the rock has been hit with tools. We look inside, squeezing our heads together. It goes down pretty deep, but we can make out a faint light inside and, for a second, the figure of my uncle swinging on his rope across the narrow field of vision, about sixty or seventy feet below us.

"It's probably a ventilation shaft", I say to Danny, "for a coal mine. My uncle said there were stairs inside, right? Wasn't that what he said?"

"Yeah, I think so."

"Wow. This is so cool!"

Thomas can hear the distant sounds of voices being carried down from above. There's suddenly more light in the cave that isn't coming from a headlamp, as if something got moved off another entrance. I look up. Sure enough, one of the eye sockets of the skull above is admitting a thin beam of daylight. Danny Stillman's face pokes into the hole and I distinctly hear him shout a greeting to the "Grand Wizard", which is what he's been calling me ever since the lunchtime conversation freshman year where he learned from me that "Wizard" carries negative connotations in some circles because it's a title used by the KKK.

I'm almost at the wooden stairs, just another stretch away. There are decent handholds right where I am. If I can just reach a little further…

I leap and feel timber in each hand as I reach the side wall. And it comes off in my hands. Rotten through. I realize in the moment that it's a lot older than I had guessed. This isn't an industrial-scale mine from the 1890s. It's older than that.

Kate watches in horror as the rope I'm tied to jerks wildly. Mr. Kretschak is definitely dangling in the air again, there's no arguing with the feeling of his entire weight pulling at my hips from thirty feet away, but what in the heck is he trying to do? For the first time, I can believe he's related to Ricky. I had expected him to be a lot more careful. It feels like he's treating the whole thing as a game.

And that's when I realize what's wrong. The rope has caught on the edge of the rock where the sloping floor gives way to the vertical passage. It's going to get cut if he makes too many more sudden moves.

"Sep, get my pack! What metal items are in that compartment?"

September snaps out of ditz mode to quickly find a few climbing cams and hexes. "Tell me what to do with these."

Not daring to let Pedro let go of me, since even at the same height I'm down more than seventy pounds on Mr. Kretschak, I get September and Jarri to jab the gear into any crack they can find in the rock. I'm going in after Mr. Kretschak. There's no choice. If I do this right, I won't need the cams to hold my weight. But I can't take any chances.

Thomas is suddenly aware of how much trouble I've got myself into. The sound of a rope cutting is the worst thing I can imagine. I scramble to grab hold of something on the wall, now keenly aware of the twenty-foot gap at my back. What was I thinking? I'm supposed to be the role model here. Act like an adult. Okay, don't panic. Those stairs aren't going to hold my weight. What else is there? There's a section of wall that looks knobby enough to my left. If I can swing myself over...

Ricky realizes that his uncle is in trouble. I lean away from the hole where I'm watching, wanting to let in as much light as possible. Just how far down is the cave bottom, I wonder? If it's really an old mine, it probably gets a lot deeper still. He's got to get out of here quick. But what can I do?

Danny the dumb kid demonstrates quite capably what *not* to do. I cannot believe that he's standing uphill from the ventilation shaft that we found, tossing stones. That nobody by the other entrance can see him is more believable.

"What the hell are you doing?", I hiss at him.

"Trying to see if I can hit the edge of the hole there. Watch this."

And just like that, a stone the size of a fist is flying through the air, before I can stop it, and goes straight down the middle of the ventilation shaft.

Kate is about to reach over to Thomas and clip him to her better-anchored end of the rope. He's still ten feet away. The rope is holding. I can reach him.

The stone nearly hits me, bouncing with an incredible crack off the rope six inches from my head. "ROCK!", I yell, the only way to alert Mr. Kretschak. It's too late for him to move entirely out of the way, and his headlamp flies off his head and down into the darkness. Somehow it didn't make any noise until the moment of impact. I am taken so terribly by surprise that I lose my grip with my left hand, which in turn makes both my feet lose their footing. My right arm can just barely handle all of my weight, and I scramble for a hold with my left hand. Thrashing blindly, my hand grabs the worst thing it could.

Mr. Kretschak's rope.

The tearing sound as the weakened rope severs is horrifying. I expect to see my teacher plunging to his death as I look down, aghast as I realize it was my fault we tried this at all.

But he's still there, firmly gripping the rocks.

"Get out of here!", he yells at me.

I start to protest, but he cuts me off.

"Go!"

Making him spend any more energy on words would be tantamount to killing him, so I pull my way up to the ledge and back up into the world outside the cave. I don't even notice Pedro and September unclipping me and trying to get the rope to where Mr. Kretschak can use it. Instead, I notice Mr. Kretschak's hand slowly reaching up above the threshold of the cave entrance.

He free-climbed his way back up. I gain a newfound respect for the man.

His feelings toward me, by contrast, haven't improved. We walk back to the campground in silence.

There's a campfire going by now and the sun is slipping toward the west as the expedition returns. **Ricky** is in a quandary. If I don't rat on Danny, my uncle will continue to think it was an accident or happenstance that sent the rock crashing down toward him. If I expose the fool-of-a-Took, I can't begin to guess how much shit he's going to be in this time. I also don't know if anybody will believe that it was him and not me.

I say nothing.

Pedro is just glad nobody got hurt. I want to enjoy the evening and campfire, so it doesn't bother me if we just sort of pretend the expedition didn't happen. Willy, Chase, and Trent are tossing around a Frisbee as Lily, Brandon, and Miss Stillman read books by the firelight, sitting on logs or stumps they must have gathered into a ring. I join the latter group, though without a book. Somehow I didn't bring one on the trip.

It's Kate, who also doesn't have a book along, who notices what Lily's reading. "*The Invisible Man.* Brandon was reading that earlier."

This is to me, I realize. Kate's sitting down on the log next to me, making me wonder if my high hopes might actually be founded.

"It's a good book." I hope that was the right thing to say.

Brandon answers, though. "I just got done with it. It really spoke to me."

Is it just me, or are his eyes glowing red in the firelight? I try not to stare, but he notices. And his eyes are definitely red or pink.

"Took my contacts out. They don't do anything for vision. I wear blue so people don't notice."

"So pink is really your natural eye color?"

"Comes with being an albino. Technically, you're supposed to say 'person with albinism' but I'm one and I couldn't care less."

Brandon the bookworm is an albino. I really didn't notice. I thought he was just a pasty blond kid who never got any fresh air.

"So", Kate asks, "are you going to try to turn invisible like in the book?"

Brandon laughs it off. I put it together right at that moment that H.G. Wells' title character finds a way to take his albinism a step further and become totally translucent.

"That wouldn't work in real life. The only invisible animals that really exist are things that live in caves where there's no light, and even those are visible if you…"

He trails off, and we all suddenly realize what he's saying. Lily puts the book down. Miss Stillman gasps.

Nobody says it. If you look through two lenses or panes of glass at the right distance, normally it focuses light and makes things look bigger or closer. Might it also focus enough light to make the invisible visible?

That's what I'm thinking, and it's what Brandon's thinking, and I'm pretty sure it's what Kate's thinking, but it's not what Miranda's thinking, I realize.

"My inhaler! I left it at Seneca Rocks. I've got to get it back before I go to sleep."

"Well, isn't that a fine kettle of fish!" blurts out Mr. Kretschak behind me.

"Miss Stillman, are you sure it's there? You don't have a backup here?"

"No, Kate, I don't. I only brought the one along. Yeah, I know it was stupid. No, you don't have to tell me."

I doubt anyone's thinking that was stupid. As far as I knew, an inhaler was like a pair of glasses, where most people who have them just have one. But I don't have asthma, so I'm not really the person to ask.

Mr. Kretschak sighs deeply. "Fine, I'll go get it. Do you

remember exactly where it is?"

"Don't worry. I'll go get it myself."

"You can't drive if you're at risk for an attack!"

"That's not a law!"

Mr. Kretschak is getting more tense by the moment, while Miss Stillman, the one who's actually in potential danger, is perfectly calm. Then again, which of them just had to free-climb out of a cave?

"I can't send you off alone on a forty-five-minute drive by yourself, and we can't both leave. I'm going. Try not to have an attack for an hour and a half."

I follow Mr. Kretschak as he turns to the van. "Wait just a second, Mr. Kretschak. Can't someone go with her? You don't have to do this."

"Alvarez", he says in that condescending tone of his, "I appreciate your initiative, but we have to follow protocol."

"Like climbing into that cave without permits or all the proper gear."

"Well, look how that almost ended! We follow the rules from now on. I don't know what I was thinking."

"I don't think there's a rule that you have to go charging off..."

Mr. Kretschak looks almost explosive. "Look, Pedro, I can't send someone who could have an asthma attack off to drive, there's nothing any of you little rats would be able to do if she had a problem while driving..."

"There is too! I'm CPR certified. Several of us are."

"I'm going right now and that's final. All you're doing is wasting valuable time!"

"I could go get it."

"I'm the adult here."

"I'm eighteen. I've got my paperwork filed, I drove yesterday and this morning…"

"Stop it now! I'm the adult in charge and you're wasting my time!"

I can't stop. My blood is up. I'm sick of being treated like I belong in the same boat as people like Willy.

"I'm trying to help out! I'm probably going to be valedictorian, you know…"

"Not if you keep this up!"

He slams the door in a huff and drives off so fast I realize he already had the ignition turned on. Off he goes, racing in the dark down the dirt road. I hope and pray he doesn't get into an accident. That's just what we need.

Ricky watches as my uncle drives off into the dark woods. I have no idea what could make him suddenly have to leave, and in such a hurry. The lights of his vehicle fade as the sounds of the engine are completely swallowed up by the forest. It's surprisingly dark, I realize. The sun is down, leaving a patchwork of pink and blue that's turning darker and darker. But I can't make myself go back to the camp and have to think about whether to tell on Danny.

I keep walking around in the woods, trying to distract myself. Gradually it occurs to me that I've succeeded. I have no idea where I am. The sky above me is dark, even though there aren't many clouds. I pull out my phone, which doesn't light up anything for more than a few feet in front of me. If someone's really going to invent a way to put a flashlight in a phone in a few years, I think that's a great idea.

By now I'm not even sure which way I went. We got back to the campsite after the incident with the cave, I grabbed a snack, and then I went off to wander in the woods. Now I'm about to get lost and end up spending the whole night in the woods.

Man, that sounds like something Danny would do.

Or Willy. Last year when we were freshmen, he ditched class once and rode a bike around the school fields with a big orange traffic cone on his head. Because he's weird.

But me? Most of my grades match my middle initial (Richard David Kretschak, after my grandfather and father), but I think I have decent street smarts. I'm not an idiot.

Or am I?

I feel like one right now. But I don't call out and hope someone hears me, because I really hope I can just find my way back by myself before anyone notices I'm missing.

What was that noise behind me?

I spin around, wishing my phone was brighter. Nothing. All that I can see are trees in every direction, other than the gentle slope of the mountain. The campfire has got to be toward the bottom, right? It has to…but I don't see it.

I look upward and see a plane flying distantly overhead. Not much good there. Only a few stars visible, and none of them are the Big Dipper. There's no moon anywhere. I start to feel like I'm surrounded by inky darkness. Should I move around or hold still? I don't want to twist my ankle again; it got injured competing in cross-country last year and reinjuring it would risk missing my next season.

Oh my God. There's that noise again. The faint crackling of dry leaves, the crack of a twig – there's something or somebody sneaking up toward me.

I run. I flip out, panic, and run through the woods, not caring what direction I go it. There are small rocks everywhere. I try to dodge them. I can see by my phone…no, not anymore. I dropped my phone. I keep running. This can't be happening. I'm going to be so mad when it turns out that it's just a raccoon.

But it sounds a lot bigger than a raccoon, even though I can't see a blasted thing. Then the rock comes, the one I didn't see. I fall headlong into the underbrush. The sound of something running toward me is overpowering. I open my mouth and scream. Barely any sound comes out. My voice cracks with fear. I pull myself up. It doesn't feel like I broke or twisted anything. I can still run.

I hear a whistling noise coming through the trees, at head level. Something's moving fast. It's an inanimate sound. I turn my head to look. I never see what hits me square between the eyes.

The Frisbee lands in **Brandon**'s hand, thrown from Trent. They let me join their game – Willy, Danny, Sep and him – once I decided I was done with reading for the night. The book I'm getting through is really frustrating me. I thought I knew who the main character was, and now he just got his head chopped off. I'm not sure I want to finish the story, because how can the ending be good?

I throw the Frisbee to Danny, who drops it, curses, and runs to pick it up. It lands at Jarri's feet as he comes back into the woods, his face looking like ash.

"Did nobody hear that except me?"

"Hear what?", we all ask.

"It sounded like someone screamed. Off in the woods."

"A guy scream or a girl scream?" Trent, of course. He's such a sexist jerk. I hate him.

"I would guess a guy. But I went to go investigate, and I didn't see anything."

We now see Jarri's holding a flashlight.

"It's *really* dark out there, you know. Can't tell from here with the fire and the lanterns, but it's basically pitch black out there. Tonight or tomorrow or yesterday is a new moon."

He looks at us expectantly.

"Yeah, so it's really dark. I get it." Which I do. Anyone walking around with dark enough clothing would be practically invisible out there, I realize.

"New moons are the times that the boundary between the land of the living and the land of the dead becomes thin", Jarri explains, "and here we are, on a new moon, in a dark forest, with a cave nearby. Here's the best part: I found korsikko markings on a whole bunch of trees out there."

For all the books I've read, I get the gist of what he's saying but "korsikko markings" totally loses me.

"Um, Jarri, what are you talking about?"

"You've been playing too many silly video games, dude." That's Trent...I'm going to kill this arrogant prick sooner or later. Why does he have to run people down all the time?

Willy, of all people, comes to Jarri's defense. "Holy Cow, Trent, you play video games all the time!"

"Yeah, I play *good* games! Guns and stuff. I bet you play a bunch of fantasy crap, don't you, Jarri?"

I jump in, and so does September. "Fantasy games are good!"

"Didn't you ever play Zelda? I still do once in a while!"

Trent just ignores us and throws Danny the Frisbee. I walk away, Jarri and September following. We head back to the campfire that Miss Stillman, Pedro, Lily, and Kate are still sitting around. Pedro's talking to the others, who are listening intently. As we approach, we realize Chase is there too, almost hidden by the big log he's leaning against.

"So what are Corsica markings?", I ask Jarri as we pull up.

"Korsikko. People mark trees with them near graveyards. A funeral procession will put a few marks on trees to signal the dead person's ghost that they shouldn't try to wander around."

"So it's like a containment sign?" September asks the question I'm also thinking.

"Yeah. I guess I just realized people don't do that here. It's a Finnish thing."

We grow silent as we sit down around the ring and listen to Pedro. He sounds very serious, and everyone else is hanging on his words.

"That was when the bombs started falling. We had to leave, and quickly. Really, we should have left in September, but how could we know it was going to be dangerous for us? We were Americans. We were supposed to be safe.

"The day that we were supposed to evacuate, my dad came into my room with a suitcase and told me to pack in ten minutes. I tried, but seriously, what twelve-year-old kid can hurry like that? I was trying to fit this toy I'd had since we moved there, a Greek chariot like Alexander the Great might have ridden when he marched in, into my suitcase, when suddenly there was this huge *boom*. Like nothing I'd ever heard before.

"Somehow I got outside the house without my suitcase. I could see my parents and the other staff all around me, running toward the helicopter we were supposed to take. All the grownups made it on. They must have thought I was on too. I will never forget the feeling of that bird lifting off into the sky, leaving me standing on the ground watching my world fly away.

"I figured they'd come back for me soon, but they kept flying away. Then our house fell down in a huge heap of dust and rubble. We'd got out of there just in time. I ran and ran and ran until I was in an alley I recognized. It was only then that I realized I still had the chariot in my hand. That and my canteen. Ever since I drank the water of Cano Cristales when I was seven, that canteen's been with me and I'm never letting it get lost."

Here Pedro pauses and takes a sip.

"Anyway, before long I realized everybody around thought I was just one more orphaned kid. I look enough like the locals that I blended in, and I had learned a little bit of Pashto. Somehow I got by. I saw things nobody should ever have to see, things I still can't talk about. So much fear. So much death. Never knowing who you could trust or who would turn you over to the Taliban for a sex slave. It happened to so many kids. By the time I saw Northern Alliance fighters shooting Taliban like they were rabid dogs, I couldn't feel any pity for them. I was just glad someone killed them before one of them got me."

We can all see Chase's look of particular horror as Pedro recounts his near brushes with a fate worse than death. What, I wonder, happened to Chase before he came to our school, that could possibly compare with getting caught in a war zone?

"It was almost five months before they finally found me and brought me back to my parents. They'd given me up for dead. The day I saw them again, at that army camp, my mom quit her Foreign Service job and vowed she'd never drag us to another country again. We moved to Cincinnati and they vowed from now on I'd have as normal an American childhood as possible."

Nobody knows what to say, except Kate.

"Do you wish your mom hadn't been in the Foreign Service then? I can't believe they'd have her take you along to Afghanistan."

"Well, if she hadn't done the service, she wouldn't have been posted in Colombia and met my dad, so I would never have been born. I wouldn't have minded going back to Colombia, that's my real home, but it's been five years that we've lived in America and I'm starting to get used to it finally."

"That makes two of us", puts in Jarri.

"But I do want to make sure if I ever have kids, they've been to Colombia before they're nine. That's how old I was when I left, and it made me who I am. More than Afghanistan, more than Ohio."

*****

Of course there's no moon tonight, thinks **Thomas** to himself as the van winds around another twist in the dirt road. I can't believe I'm driving back to Seneca Rocks in the dark. Miranda's inhaler had so better be there when I arrive, and it had better be on a picnic table like she thinks and not dropped somewhere on one of the trails. I'm so angry right now, I can't even think straight.

It's David's fault, all of it. Why does he have to ruin everything? Why does my *perfect* brother have to cast a shadow over every nice thing I try to do and turn it into something ugly? I never wanted to run down a good kid like Alvarez or Bauer the way I've been doing. What have I become? Another judgmental, power-hungry teacher like my brother?

Oh shit, is that a deer in the road?

I swerve to miss it, and misjudge the sharpness of the curve. The van immediately goes off the road, and next thing I know I'm down the hill. It's not rolling, just driving uncontrollably through underbrush. I have to find a way to stop it. The brakes fail. This is impossible. What the hell is going on? I pull the emergency brake. The van still doesn't stop, not until I'm at the bottom of the valley, at least two hundred feet below the road I just fell off of. For all the crashing down the hill I've just done, I don't feel too bad. Nothing's broken, not even the windshield. I'm going to be okay, once I get my breath back.

The van has come to a complete stop in a clearing. There's no light at all except for the one I click on above my head. I open the door and get ready to step out to see how badly damaged the van is.

And then the ground disappears under me. The van crashes straight through the ground, taking me down with it. We must have landed on the roof of some kind of pit, like a sinkhole that hadn't quite opened up yet. It's so fast that I don't get to complete another thought before everything is swallowed up in utter blackness.

8: JUSTICE

December 2007
Northern Virginia

"I did exactly as you instructed."

Oake looked like he was about to say more, but the five people staring at him from around the boardroom table glared him into silence. He clenched his jaw and glared back, focusing his gaze not on the five accusers but on the only person standing other than himself.

Flandell sighed and broke the uncomfortable silence. Hiring Oake had been a mistake. Twenty-three years old with a college degree in Criminal Justice – not from one of the many reputable Criminal Justice programs, but from a big state school where that was the generic major for kids who still hadn't figured out anything they were good at by the end of sophomore year – and with an attitude that made him seem more like a criminal than a just person, Carter Oake had made it through a small part of police officer training before psychological testing indicated he would not be courteous or responsible in the line of duty. He was one of thousands, Flandell thought sometimes, of thuggish young white men tucked away in different rough corners of America who had the aggression to be soldiers but not the discipline, and the toughness to be cops but not the basic decency needed to serve and protect. Many ended up in prison, some as inmates and others as guards. This one got to work for a branch of the United States government, although now Flandell and her colleagues needed to figure out if he still should.

"Oake, your instructions were very clear. Keep the situation under wraps. No publicity. Nobody asking questions. We gave you a very specific *meth*od to accomplish your objective [everyone noticed how she stressed the first syllable of "method", and Ovenden barely suppressed a chuckle] in the cleanest, swiftest manner possible. You made things worse than if we hadn't sent you at all! Now we've got all those reporters out there asking questions that could mean a federal investigation!"

Flandell paused to take a breath. Nobody interrupted. Then she pounded the table so hard as she spoke that the entire tabletop shook. Remstine's bottled water tipped over and poured onto the floor. People clutched instinctively at the papers in front of them.

"*We*'re the ones who do investigations, damn it! If Congress or another agency decides we've been misusing taxpayer funds…"

"Well", said Ylonen hesitantly, "technically, we…"

"None of this ever happened! There's nothing down there, there is no site at all, and nobody ever went poking around anywhere! That's what we needed. We're finished unless this all goes away immediately. That's been impossible ever since those kids got killed."

"*IF* I may interject", came the voice of the person standing next to Oake, "you people interfered with a delicate and sensitive mission that wouldn't have harmed anyone or broken any laws. If your goon had stayed out of it, no one would ever have come near the site!"

As soon as he had said it, he realized something didn't add up. "How did you even know…"

Remstine curtly told him how.

The man threw up his hands in frustration. "Ridiculous!"

He looked like he was about to say more, but Flandell cut him off. "If it wasn't for you, this leak would never have happened in the first place. You have nothing else to say to this panel." She turned to the four people at the table with her. "It's time for damage control. The scales have tipped too far, and something has to be jettisoned from this side to make them balance."

Oake, at six-three and two-hundred-fifty the most intimidating of the three men in the room, glared at the other man, then at the occupants of the table. He looked almost predatory as he stared at them one by one, sizing up how much bigger he was than each of the four women and the man whose stature matched his surname, "Little". If they fired him, he wouldn't go on to try and find another job. He'd go to prison for killing at least one or two of them.

"And I suppose that's me, huh? Make me take the fall for doing the unpleasant job you set me up with?"

Flandell shook her head. "Not you. Him."

She pointed to the other standing man, who first glared back and then gasped in shock. "You can't! Do you have any idea the kind of authority I…"

But she just cut him off and finished his sentence. "…pretended to have? Claimed for yourself? I've never heard of someone as sleazy as you in all my years in Washington!"

"How am I any different from you?!", he shot back.

It was Remstine who spoke, firmly but with almost impossible civility. "This agency acts on behalf of the United States government. We hide things that the public is not ready to know about. This operation has been going since the Zachary Taylor administration and we are not about to let it fail now because of a few meddling civilians. There will be no story. The Heart of the Raven stays buried where it belongs until the occasion of genuine need. What happened will be explained as the result of a madman sending a bunch of dumb kids on a treasure hunt and setting them up for disaster, which has the benefit of being true."

The finality in her voice was unmistakable. Only Ovenden and Ylonen weren't satisfied. It was the former who spoke, her voice hushed so that only the occupants of the table could hear.

"He's already lost a child. Isn't that punishment enough?"

"It's not enough to stop the media. He takes the blame, our hands are clean and we go on with our work."

As they filed out of the room, Ovenden glared at Oake, only three years younger than herself, as she noticed the look of triumph on his brutish face.

"Wipe that smile off your face, Carter. You're not going to get out of this scot-free. I'm going to destroy your career if it's the last thing I do."

9: HERMIT

It's very late at night now. The fire has dwindled to a small flicker no brighter than a candle. Sunrise won't come for another four hours, long enough that we could still get a little bit of sleep if we all went to bed now. But nobody has. We're afraid that Mr. Kretschak won't come back. **Miranda** more than anyone else.

I know for a fact that I left my inhaler at Seneca Rocks, the kind of thing that you'd expect a kid to do. Danny has left his retainer behind at so many restaurants that our parents wish he still had braces on. I'm kicking myself. Here I'm supposed to be the responsible adult, setting a good example for these helpless kids, and it feels like Kate and Pedro are better prepared for life than I am.

The kids are sitting around the flickering fire, nobody bothering to put more wood on it. I think we're all hoping Mr. Kretschak will come back momentarily; I for one have been hoping this for about three hours. If only there was a way to figure out where he is. Obviously we've called him, but getting a signal meant a potentially perilous walk to the top of the nearest hill and his phone went straight to voicemail. At least everyone is around. I think.

I do a head count again. Only ten students. This is no different from taking roll when I get called on to cover an unfamiliar class for an absent colleague. I try again. Kate, Lily, and September are present; it's a boy who's missing, imagine my surprise. Pedro's here, Willy, Chase, Brandon, oh my fricking god stop moving around, okay that's Jarri, there's Trent, my idiot brother is right there, shoot, who does that leave?

That's when I realize there is still a way to find them. The vans have a paired GPS system that tells the occupants of one vehicle where the other one is. We even got it set up so that the van GPS can find the students through their cell phones, although not all of the kids signed up for it. I just have to get into the van.

Getting up gently and breathing deeply, I walk toward the van and hit the "unlock" button on the clicker. It doesn't work. I open the door manually with the key, wondering what people in another decade will do once they stop making actual keys for cars. Electronic clickers don't last forever, do they? This one obviously didn't.

I climb into the driver's seat and power on the GPS. It has nine minutes of battery life remaining. I fumble through the commands, my pride not letting me call one of the more tech-savvy kids like Jarri for help, and find the function for locating the other vehicle. It doesn't do anything for a few frustrating seconds as I wonder what I'm doing wrong.

Then it displays a location a quarter mile away from the road. The topographic map shows that Thomas' tracker is hundreds of feet below the elevation of the road. I stare in dismay at the display, hoping I'm misinterpreting it but knowing I'm reading it exactly right. The signal flickers, and a little "help" balloon pops up saying that there's a weak connection at the other end.

I try finding the kids' cell phones, wondering if one of them is not around. A handful of balloons pop up close to my location, as I'd expected. Nothing anywhere else. Maybe one of the boys did finally go to bed and is just in his tent.

Pedro and Kate should see this, I realize, taking the GPS out of the van and bringing it up to the campfire circle. As I'd hoped, Kate and Pedro sit down near me so that we're in a circle. I show them what I'm seeing.

"Not much battery life left. We should get it charged. Can we turn the van on?" That's Kate. Practical as always. Why didn't I think of that?

It doesn't matter, though. The van doesn't start. I let Pedro try; it still doesn't start. Kate tries. Same result.

"Who knows anything about cars?", I ask the group of sleepy teens, not knowing if any of them will respond.

Jarri hesitantly raises his hand. "I can take a look."

"You know", says Trent, "it's Ricky who really knows about cars…wait a second, where is he?"

I know in a flash that's who my head count didn't show. With only a few minutes left on the GPS, I try the last function again. This time it shows one dot over a mile away in the woods, toward the north. The direction we came from twelve hours ago and in which Thomas drove off. Sure enough, it's Ricky's number. Did he ride with his uncle? I'm sure I remember seeing him since then, but now I'm doubting everything I was sure about.

Jarri looks at the GPS. "I might be able to charge it from my music player. Can I take a look?"

I let him have it. He looks at it, confused, then blurts out what I'm still not sure I should share with the kids. "Ricky's out in the woods! When was the last time we saw him?"

Lily shakes her head. "He's not out in the woods. Look at his tent."

We look at the small red tent. Something moves inside it, not a whole lot of movement, but clearly that of a person rolling over in his sleep.

"Okay", I say, "so it's not Ricky, it's his phone that's out there. His uncle probably grabbed it by mistake. He must be walking back from the crash site…but he's going in the wrong direction…"

I realize too late I've let the cat out of the bag.

"Crash? What crash?"

I shush them all. "The GPS looks like Mr. Kretschak's vehicle crashed off of the road. It's down at the bottom of a hill. I think we need to get a few hours of rest and start finding our bearings in daylight. It's only going to get worse if we run around in the dark…"

Then I cough. And wheeze and gasp for breath. It's happening. Oh fuck. Not now. It can't be…

Kate is the first to Miss Stillman's side as she collapses to the ground in a sitting position, trying to stay up straight and breathe deeply. It looks like a bad attack. Her eyes are rolling back in her head and her limbs are quivering. Does she have something worse than asthma?

"What do we do?!" That's September, panicking just when we need everyone to be calm.

"Give her some space! Nobody say anything. I've got this. You're going to be okay, Miranda." It seems more natural to use her real name given that she was only my age when I was in middle school. "Stay with me. Breathe."

Pedro knows I have to do something. Kate can keep Miss Stillman from getting into serious trouble, but the rest of the kids need to be kept occupied and there's no way they'll go to sleep now. We've got to get in touch with Mr. Kretschak. I try calling his phone. No signal. I remember he's got Ricky's phone and is probably trying to walk back here from the crashed van.

"Jarri, can I take a look at the GPS again? Show me where the other van is."

"I wish I could. When I went back to that function, it just said the other unit has run out of battery and switched itself off. I have no idea where it is."

"But it's got to be somewhere on the road going north. Where's the signal from Ricky's phone?"

Jarri flips back to the phone-finder. "He's a mile and a half due north of us, going east. We've got to call him ASAP."

Woo-oo-oo-ump. The GPS runs out of its last battery reserves and shuts off. I *love* how technology is failing us. Van won't start, GPS is dead, phones can't get a signal. Maybe we need to go back up to the hill. Mr. Kretschak, with Ricky's phone, might be high enough up that he can get a signal and we can reach him. I hope he at least has the inhaler.

Time to get control of the group. "If you can hear me, please clap one time." A few people do. "If you can hear me, please clap twice." More claps. "If you can hear me, please clap three times."

The sound gets everyone else's attention. I need to act swiftly.

"Miss Stillman, can you hear what I'm saying?" She nods. "Kate, are you alright with staying here? Danny, Lily, stay with them. Sep, Chase, Willy, you guys look exhausted. Get to sleep right away. Trent, I need you with me. Jarri, Brandon, you too."

To my relief, everyone agrees. Trent comes up to me, looking more serious than I've ever seen him before.

"What do we need to do?"

Five minutes later, we're heading uphill in the woods, setting a course for northeast. Trent keeps pace with me easily, and for the first time I realize that for all his immaturity he has real potential as a leader. This guy could be valedictorian a year and a half from now if he had any self-control. At a time like this, he's snapped out of the hooligan act. Jarri and Brandon aren't in as good of physical condition – too much time sitting in front of a desk, I suppose – but they hustle along, keeping their eyes out for signs of Mr. Kretschak. There's no sign of Jarri's headphones.

Every hundred feet or so, I try my phone. We've agreed that it's better to try one phone rather than have everyone try at the same time, so that the faint signal doesn't get divided too thinly to use. On the ninth attempt, I get a signal and call Ricky's phone.

Duh-daw-BLEETNGK! The decidedly unpleasant atonal noise of the error message sounds so much louder here in the dark remote woods at two or three in the morning than it normally does. I hope sooner or later they'll phase out that sound.

"YOUR CALL CANNOT BE COMPLETED AS DIALED. PLEASE TRY AGAIN LATER."

"We don't have 'later'!" I shout into the phone. "Damn it! We've got to climb higher up."

I fold the phone closed, but as I do this, the background of my wallpaper jumps out at me. It's a stock photo of four golden retriever puppies playing in a haystack, but viewed from a high angle where every pixel of the screen looks a different color from normal, the image suddenly looks freaky. The puppies still have light faces and dark eyes and noses, but for just an instant they look like ghoulish fiends. Almost, I realize, like a half-invisible human-dog hybrid. Trent and Brandon are close enough to me that they see the image too.

Brandon gasps involuntarily. "That's just what it looked like!" The words are out of my mouth before I can stop them. "You've got to believe me. I saw something like that out the window of the van last night at the campground."

"When was this?" Pedro is brought up short just before he's about to charge off again.

"I think you had just gone to bed. The idiots – no offense, Trent – were about to go do their shenanigans, I was in the van reading, and I looked out the window and there it was, not two feet away. As tall as any of you guys, with the face of a dog, standing on its back legs. It was so pale, except for its nose and eyes."

Pedro has to think about it. My mind is churning. A human body with the head of a dog. When I was in Afghanistan, my tutor, Omar, fired up my imagination with tales of dog-headed men that many ancient Greeks believed lived in Afghanistan and neighboring countries. The eccentric, hermit-like old man spoke so excitedly when telling such tales that I still think he might have believed them himself. I never found out what happened to Omar when the war broke out. I hope he's alright.

"How long did you see it?"

"Just for a second. I jumped back because I was so startled and it disappeared."

I think about it as we keep walking.

"Did you have your glasses on?"

"Yeah, I did...two panes of glass. My glasses and the window of the van. Remember what the gas station owner said?"

We all do. Trent scoffed then, but now he looks serious and so does Jarri.

"Jarri", says Trent, "didn't you say something earlier about the boundary between the land of the living and the land of the dead?"

"Yeah, I did. I didn't think you were listening. He was, though." He nods toward Brandon.

"Because", Trent continues, "when I think of a guy with a dog head, I'm right back to second grade when we did a unit on ancient Egypt. Anubis. That's his name, right? The god of the dead?"

"That's a jackal head…" I start, but realize the difference is insignificant.

"What have we got ourselves into?" Brandon looks really worried. Not that the rest of us don't, I guess.

Out of force of habit, for the first time on the trip I reach my hand to the St. Christopher medallion around my neck and stroke it a few times. The patron saint of travelers has always resonated more with me than the saint whose name I bear. I lost my original necklace in Afghanistan, but got this one shortly after I moved to Cincinnati.

It dawns on me, uncomfortably, that Christopher is one of a very few saints who sometimes appears in icons with a canine head.

Brandon's brain is pounding more than my heart as we charge up the hill. Surely there's got to be a decent signal up here. I'm not built for this kind of thing. I sit in a chair and read books. They take me away from real life with all its pressures and off to places where I can imagine wanting to live. Granted, I'm not so sure about the latest book I've been reading, but in a few years they're probably going to make a bunch of movies about it and it will be nice to have already read the books.

There's a kid in that book who has my name. I had never realized that my name probably means "raven" in Welsh until I got to the note someone had scribbled in the margins of a scene where this kid starts having dreams about three-eyed ravens. From other books I've read, I'm starting to think that this fictional Brandon is a shaman; sometimes, I wonder if that's really my calling too. I have to put all of my bookish knowledge to use someday, but the thought of spending my life writing research papers scares me. Holing up in a library doesn't bother me. I can't write to save my life, and that part of academic life makes me wonder what other kinds of hermit-like careers exist in real life.

After what seems like forever, Pedro stops and tries again. He dials Ricky's number and waits…and waits…and yells at the phone.

"This *is* an emergency call!"

"Try calling 911!" suggests Trent. "If it's bad enough with Miss Stillman…"

"Okay, sure!" Pedro hangs up and is about to dial when we hear a distinct groan coming from only a short distance away.

"Hold that thought. Let's get a grip on the situation before we go making a call."

Jarri and Trent shine their flashlights toward the source of the sound. There's a man lying prone about twenty feet away, to the left of the route we took here from camp, covered in mud, his head and one hand raised toward us.

"Helppp…" comes the dull croak of his voice, sounding like rusty hinges.

This is when I wake up, right? This can't be happening.

It's real, though. **Trent** and Jarri trade glances uneasily and I know we're both thinking of Kate's stunt yesterday. Could this be something like that? I don't recognize this guy. In the beam of my flashlight, it looks like he's missing several teeth. His hair is long and scraggly. He looks genuinely desperate.

"Can we get him back to camp?", asks Brandon.

None of us know what will happen once we do, but we can certainly carry him.

10: WHEEL

October 1, 1849

The subterranean space was truly a thing of magnificent splendor, Edgar thought for the third time today. If the old legends were true, and a secretive race of wise beings dwelt somewhere in the chthonic depths, spinning the threads of fate, they probably lived in a place like this. He couldn't help grinning as they walked deeper and deeper into the cave.

Sarah grinned at him as she turned around, the light of her lantern dancing spookily across her face. Ahead of her walked Obadiah, their guide to this deep and ghastly place, and behind Edgar came the reassuring stride of Tobias, holding the third lantern. Edgar alone bore no light on this voyage. He didn't need it with such prepared and trustworthy companions.

Life had changed for the better since he'd first visited the cave, although that had only been the upper chambers. He'd lost track of the times he'd come here, sometimes with Obadiah, sometimes with Tobias, sometimes with both. They'd lead him into a space where he could feel the darkness embrace him, and at his request they'd leave. He'd sit in silence and darkness, pondering and letting go of extraneous thoughts. Stories came to him, dark stories, macabre stories, tales of terror and woe and mayhem. The darkness of the cave seeped into his brain and his fingers, and when he emerged he'd set his visions to ink on paper.

People liked his stories, at least some of them. Enough to keep a roof over his head and a stein of beer in his hand, though in truth he drank far less than everyone seemed to think of him. He'd seen what alcoholism could do to a man before, and it wasn't pretty. Not for him. His vices were of different sorts.

"This is so perfect!" Sarah beamed. They were far below her family's land up here in the western mountains, away from the urban bustle and genteel respectability of Richmond. She'd never lived here, her father being the only one out of all his brothers who'd chosen a different life than that of their Yorkshire ancestors, but even so you couldn't be a Royster of Virginia and not care for the family cave.

It was through Sarah, his childhood acquaintance and the sweetheart of his youth, that Edgar had met her cousins, Obadiah and Tobias. Tobias didn't have the Royster name since his place in the family was through his mother, but he'd been raised on these lands and knew the cave as well as anyone in the family. It was Obadiah, however, short of stature like Edgar but wiry and tough like a wolverine, who had probed its depths and gone further under the earth than any Royster in the four generations who'd lived here.

"We have to face reality", Tobias had said a week ago back in Richmond, "and the reality is that highwaymen are a thing of the past. The frontier has moved too far to the west, and we're not people of the open plains. We're people of the hill country. This is where we belong, here in Virginia. The cave has stored our family's wealth before; now it shall generate it."

Edgar had been captivated by the idea. They'd turn the cave in which Roysters of the 1820s and '30s had stored valuable goods stolen from unwary travelers into an attraction. What better place than here to recreate underworlds from the various corners of the known world? People would come here to the hamlet of Cran Ross and pay money to visit Hell, then go back and convince their neighbors they should do the same. It wouldn't be a place of torment, obviously; they'd be entertained by people dressed as devils and demons and educated by displays of underworlds from the mythologies of different cultures. Royster Cave, the place already known locally as the Dark Heart, would be both theatre and museum.

That was where Edgar came in. Obadiah Royster was a simple man, one who remembered what he learned but whose world was that of the physical dimension. Put a hammer and saw in this man's hands and give him enough wooden planks, and he would build a staircase into the very side of a cavern. Tobias handled money. Already several business ventures in Richmond had succeeded with his guidance. Now thirty-five and in the prime of life, Tobias Reynolds was ready to open a venture of his own. Sarah Elmira Royster, whom Edgar loved more than anyone or anything, even his first wife now gone from consumption, had the eye for presentation. Everywhere they went in the cave, she could see what needed to be done to it to make it accessible and attractive. She had scoped out where they should have people sit to watch a performance, where the actors who would dress as devils should wait before the audience arrived, and dozens of other details Edgar would never have wrapped his head around.

But when it came to actual content, Sarah had only some idea and her cousins none at all of what their audiences should see in the different chambers. Edgar, however, had researched old cultures in preparation for some of his books. Most of his stories had turned out to have little to do with ancient history, but even so his awareness of the Greek and Celtic and Roman and Persian and other mythologies and histories shone through his work.

He'd been preparing this for some time, before the clandestine departure from Richmond and the staged public farewell to Sarah that would keep anyone from realizing they were on this venture together. They'd already staked out a couple of underworlds in earlier chambers; one room now bore a wooden sign in a notch in the wall marking it as "Sheol", underworld of the Hebrews, another "Elysium", still another "Tuonela", land of the dead in Finnish myth.

Similar signs with other names now lay tucked under Tobias' other arm as he waited for Sarah and Edgar to settle on locations for them: Duat of the Egyptians, Karnuga of the Babylonians, Hades, Avalon, Valhalla. Edgar knew that even Tobias had never been this far deep in the cave. There was a lot to do in the higher chambers, especially the incredible spot where one could see the perfect image of a human skull leering down from the ceiling. They could surely capitalize on that one, and all the more so because not a dollar had been spent making it. The skull was completely natural.

"I've been thinking about my next story. It's kind of like where we are right now, in a cavern deep below the earth." Sarah enjoyed listening to Edgar tell about his story ideas; she'd liked it ever since those halcyon days half a life ago when they were in their first fruits of love and the world looked a bright mystery box ready for exploring. His stories had been happier then, though; life had made his outlook grim and his stories grimmer.

What a life it had been. He'd not traveled as far in space as some, but had certainly wandered the gamut of human conditions. Job after job had failed. He'd tried the military, only to be expelled from West Point, never quite knowing why. John, the man who'd given him the name "Allan" that made him sound more respectable than his name would without it, had alternately supported his dreams and cursed them. Finally, things had ended badly between Edgar and the man who had been like a father to him. He carried that guilt with him like an albatross around his neck…that was one of his favorite poems, he often thought, one that had influenced his attitude toward life.

Up and down and round and round Edgar's fortune had swung, first marrying a cousin half his age while himself a young man, then somehow staying married to her for much longer than people thought their inappropriate match could last, then grieving her after the sickness took her. He never said her name now, or even thought it. She was nevermore. That was all he would allow himself to say.

"So these travelers", he continued in his rough idea for a next story, "are deep in the earth when they come across a chamber full of diamonds. Not piled on the ground, but along the walls. The entire wall is lined with diamonds. It sparkles in the light of their torches."

"Torches? Are you setting this one in an earlier time?"

"Perhaps. I wonder if it would be more believable or less if I had it take place today. As I was saying, it's a large diamond-lined chamber. They file in, and learn that it's the home of beings who have lived here in the cave, nearly invisible, for thousands of years. I think they are descended from natives who went underground so many years ago that they've changed until they're more wolf than man."

"Oh please, Edgar! How could that ever happen?"

"You know, Sarah, there are men of learning in Europe right now who believe that our race came from the apes by a process of gradual change over a very long time. I believe sooner or later they'll touch off a right firestorm of controversy, but they're quite right. How did we create dogs from wolves, or change sheep and cattle from their wild ancestors to the docile beasts we know? Gradual change. The ones who bear the right characteristics are allowed to reproduce further, and their characteristics go on to the next generation and thus carried on further.

"But I digress. These beings, neither wolf nor man but something in between, lock the travelers into the chamber, and we think they're going to eat them. Certainly in some of my stories they would. Here, though, it turns out to be for their protection. There's some danger out there, some horrible danger, and only a chamber lined with diamonds can protect them. The danger passes, and the companions go on and return in time to the surface. But now they realize they each know a terrible secret. Can you tell me what it is?"

Sarah thought about it. "It's not because of the wolf men. It's the diamonds. There's so much wealth hidden down in the earth that they'd be rich if they ever got it up…except if they bring too much diamond up, they'd flood the market and diamonds would cease to be worth anything."

"So, how should they handle it?"

"I think the right thing for them to do would be to sit on it, waiting for a time when there are so few diamonds being dug up worldwide that prices are really low, then mine and sell enough to get rich. But, since it's one of your stories, I think they'll start killing each other to hide the knowledge."

Edgar smiled. Sarah could read his mind like a book.

"I'm trying to decide if they should all kill each other off or if one of them should survive. But yes, the knowledge will turn them against each other. So the diamonds save their lives, but then kill them. Ah, you know, if anything happens to me and I don't get around to writing the story, I hope someone else will. Surely there will be some other great writer who comes along and can tell such a story, even if it ends up being different from my idea."

Sarah laughed. "Is that what you consider yourself, a great writer?"

Edgar pretended to be affronted. "Why not?"

"You're forty years old, just coming into your prime. Wait at least another ten before you try to claim greatness."

Something in her tone made Edgar suddenly less lighthearted.

They walked in silence until Obadiah stopped at the edge of a deep chasm. Sarah, Edgar, and then Tobias branched out along the ledge, which was wider than the passage they'd just come through. Daring himself to look, Edgar peered over the edge.

At first he saw nothing, but then as Sarah held her lantern out, Edgar thought it looked like there was water at the bottom. A small trickle of water, not a true stream like the one in one of the upper caverns, he would have guessed, but it was hard to judge in the dim light just how far down the chasm went.

"How far down are we?", he asked.

Obadiah shrugged. "Really far."

"More than a thousand feet down", Tobias ventured. "I doubt even the greatest men of learning in Philadelphia or Paris have instruments that would tell us for certain. Still, we are well above sea level, I can assure you of that. The ground above us is quite higher up than we have descended.

Obadiah grunted. "Like I said, really far."

Sarah set down her pack and pulled out some rope and crampons. "Let's cross! It's only ten feet or so to the other side, and look, that passage goes onward."

None of the men were about to disagree, so they all started pulling out their ropes and tools. The set-up was different from descending a sheer face, Edgar knew that much, but he left the specifics to the Royster cousins. All of them, even Richmond-bred

Sarah, knew more about this sort of thing than he ever would. His research sometimes led him to understand things his education had never raised, like how a pendulum could be made to descend slightly with each swing, or how long it took for one person to build a small brick wall, but so far none of his characters had need to cross a chasm deep in a cavern using only rope.

Edgar had thought they might construct a simple bridge, but instead Obadiah and Tobias rigged up an elaborate system with rope clipped firmly to the floor in no fewer than four places, strengthened by additional supports on the cavern wall behind them and several feel below the ledge. All four spelunkers now had rope firmly tied around their waists, linked to the firm supports and to each other. It seemed like overkill, thought Edgar, but what would he know?

"Edgar," said Tobias, "I want you to have the honor of crossing this chasm first. Don't worry, it's perfectly safe. You'll be firmly attached to the near side at all times."

"How do we know any of those ropes on the far side are secure? You just looped it around that stalagmite there. What if it breaks off?"

"It won't. Look."

Tobias demonstrated confidence in his setup by stepping off the edge and into the crevasse, dangling in midair from the elaborate rope system. His weight evenly distributed among the various points of contact, the entrepreneur swung himself in a full circle without holding onto anything.

"Fair enough. I just want to look at the map before I cross. Do we have any idea what's coming up?"

"Even I've never been across", said Obadiah. "I've been this far alone twice. The last time, I thought I saw something move in the tunnel on the other side. It looked like a dog. Didn't get a good look at it, though."

"Oh, is that why you want me to go first, then?"

"I'll be right there behind you, Edgar", promised Tobias. "Though to be honest, out of the gentlemen here you are the least threatening person. If the MacGregors turn out to be down here, you're not part of the Royster family and they won't treat you nearly as badly as they'd treat us. If their dogs are roaming down here, somehow I think you're less likely than Obadiah to provoke them to a fight. But honestly, I think it was a trick of the light."

"Are we under MacGregor land, then?" asked Sarah.

"I can't tell for sure," said Tobias, "but I believe the chasm may be directly under the property line. So technically, yes, we would be trespassing. It doesn't matter, though, if we have the only access."

Edgar summoned up his courage. He did not consider himself a brave man, nor had his instructors at West Point, but he could do this. Following Tobias' and Obadiah's instructions, he placed the final clip in a small fissure on the part of the rock directly overhead and swung out. Every rope held. Edgar wasted no time in scrambling to the other side.

Nothing happened. He laughed aloud with relief. No sinister alarm bell, no sudden appearance by a monstrous guardian – it was no different from anywhere else in the cave. Tobias came across soon, landing on Edgar's side as Sarah started her way over the void.

Tobias unclipped himself from the rope, wordlessly prompting Edgar to do the same. Edgar shot him a quizzical look.

"Shouldn't we wait until we're all across?"

"Obadiah's staying. Wouldn't do for us to all get stranded over here, would it?"

Edgar hadn't thought of that.

"Sarah will catch up with us. Let's get some sense of where we're going."

Taking Tobias' lantern with them, the two men set off down the tunnel and found that it turned to the left after about thirty feet.

It had been impossible to tell from across the chasm. The tunnel, now just tall enough for Edgar to stand but requiring Tobias to hunch, snaked back and forth a few times until Edgar had lost all sense of direction. He dearly hoped there was no methane deposit waiting around the next corner. They'd be blown to bits in an instant if the vapors ignited.

After several twists and turns, they stopped short and sniffed the air. There was no doubt they both smelled something. Methane, however, had no scent, exactly why it was so dangerous to miners. Here, the smell was cloying and bitterly sweet, a mix of honey and rotting flesh. Edgar froze, feeling as though ice water had been injected into all of his veins. Tobias looked nervous too.

A deathly sense of trepidation overpowering him, Edgar reached his hand against the wall. Black and sticky it came back to his hand, something smeared to it. As Tobias moved the lantern around, they could see that whatever it was coated the walls and floor of the tunnel, which had begun to slope downward. The soles of their boots were already slick with it.

A grim look passed over Tobias' face. "I don't think anything is to be gained from going further this way. Let us return to our companions."

No sooner had he said this and Edgar tacitly agreed than a scream broke out. It sounded like Obadiah. The sound of footfalls, light like Sarah's, echoed down the tunnel. Edgar, who'd studied the properties of sound for a few of his stories, was pretty sure she was running away from him and Tobias, toward the sound of Obadiah. Then an animalistic snarl broke out. Edgar was reminded of a book he'd read the previous year, imported from England, where the heroine wondered for many pages about the source of strange grunts and snarls and laughs and screams coming from the hallway of her employer's huge country manor, only to discover the master's wife is mad and locked in the attic, occasionally regaling the rest of the household with her noises. He had wished he'd thought of that idea himself upon reading it. Now, he felt like he was trapped in one of the frightening passages of that book.

They ran and arrived at the crevasse. Sarah's lantern stood a foot from the edge on the side they had crossed to, still burning steadily; she had certainly set it down with care and not dropped it. On the far side, there was no sign of Obadiah or his lantern.

"What happened?" Edgar felt frantic with worry.

"I don't know! I'm going to have a look down."

Tobias knelt and leaned over the edge of the crevasse. Barely an instant later, he screamed and flung himself backward to safety, clutching at his face as a flurry of dark wings landed on it. A raven, Edgar, thought, though it made no sense. A bat, he realized it had to be, a large bat, but he knew that in real life bats don't attack people. He moved to get a closer look and slipped, his shoes still slippery. The impact knocked Tobias' lantern from Edgar's hands and over the edge of the crack. He heard a scream that could only be Sarah.

When Edgar righted himself, whatever had been in Tobias' face was gone and they leaned back over the edge. Sarah hung by a rope, holding on only with her hands, more than ten feet down. Still no sign of Obadiah. Edgar tried to remain calm. Panic, and his beloved would surely die. Stay calm, and they might yet retrieve her.

He tried to lower himself on another rope, but Tobias stopped him. "No, Edgar, think! The whole rope system is collapsing. It must have been jostled loose, unless Obadiah left us here willingly. No, it couldn't be that. It's got to be an accident. We can't use any of these ropes or we risk straining them too much."

"But we've got to climb down to her! What else can we...?"

Edgar realized what, and didn't wait for Tobias to answer. He pulled off his coat and handed one cuff to Tobias. "Hold onto this. It's good tailoring and it should hold my weight."

Without waiting for a response, Edgar tied his shirt to the coat and then his pant leg to the free sleeve of the shirt, climbing down only in his breeches. It was fine. Sarah had seen him wearing less before, and he her; Tobias was another man, and it was an emergency anyway. He lowered himself over the edge, hoping the clothes would hold his weight.

They did. He made a mental note to praise his tailor to the sky when he returned to Richmond.

Edgar found Sarah's hand and grabbed it firmly. She was remarkably calm for someone dangling from a rope, and small enough that even a small man like him could pull her upward. Sarah's other hand let go of the rope for just long enough to reach significantly higher up. They repeated the process, each time involving a heart-stopping moment when the garments had to hold both people's weight, until Sarah could reach up to Tobias, who pulled her to safety.

As he himself climbed up, Edgar realized that Tobias had been standing firmly on his coat sleeve rather than holding it. Once again, he was glad these Royster cousins were more practical than he.

"What happened?", he and Tobias asked Sarah in unison.

"I wish I could tell you. I had just rounded a few corners when Obadiah screamed. It had to be him. I thought he'd fallen in, but then when I got here, something hit me from behind. It felt like someone was tackling me, but it couldn't have been Obadiah, can it?"

"Yet you had time to set down your lantern."

"It happened as soon as I set it down, obviously."

Edgar wasn't sure he quite believed her story. That awful feeling came back. Was the woman he loved trustworthy or not?

But if not, to what end could she possibly be deceiving him?

"There's blood running down your ankle."

Sarah looked in response to her cousin's concern, and sure enough a trickle of blood ran down the outside of her right ankle. She deftly lifted her skirt to the knee, not caring what her cousin saw, and found a cut on the outside of her knee.

"Must have scratched it when I hit the rock. Ah well, doesn't look too bad. I can wait to get it patched up until we're up at the surface."

"Assuming we can get there."

"Edgar! Don't say such a thing!"

Edgar would never forget what happened next. An arrow sang through the dim space above them and sheared cleanly through one of the ropes that still lay stretched across the crevasse.

Tobias looked haggard. "Oh God protect us. MacGregors. They've always preferred bows to guns. Typical Scottish savages."

"We have to get across now!"

It was absurd to try, but Sarah was absolutely right. Grabbing the rope she'd been hanging from, she looped it around a sturdy outcrop at one corner of the tunnel entrance and chasm wall and swung out as far as she could. Changing her grip in midair to one of the remaining ropes connected to the side they'd come from, Sarah pulled herself to the far wall of the crevasse, beneath the ledge where they had stood earlier, and started to work her way up. Another arrow flew out of the darkness above Edgar and Tobias, striking Sarah through the right knee and giving her a much worse injury than the one already there.

Edgar was amazed that Sarah didn't even scream, but he could not contain his rage. "Down here, you coward! Shoot me, not her!"

Tobias pulled him back. "Your wish will be granted!"

"I don't care!"

Straining with effort, Sarah hauled herself up to the far ledge and crawled up the tunnel. She was in the dark over there, Edgar knew. Somehow they had to get the remaining lantern across or they'd face a long walk in the dark.

Biting the handle of Sarah's lantern, he lunged from a run of two paces and launched himself into space, grabbing for a strand of rope. A third arrow flew, and for a horrible moment he thought it was all over. Then he saw nothing at all, but because the archer had gone for the lantern rather than the rope. His fingers closed around their intended target and he could feel his way upward, but the light was gone and from the feeling in his face and throat several shards of broken glass had grazed or penetrated his skin.

How quickly fortune turns, he mused bitterly. It was the last thought Edgar entertained before found his way up onto the ledge and slipped into unconsciousness in the total darkness.

11: STRENGTH

"Though fears run wild in the night, the morning brings new hope." **Pedro** repeats the mantra, thinking it's probably in the Psalms somewhere or close enough to an actual quote. I'm hoping and praying that the sunlight will bring an end to this weirdness.

But, drama is never in short supply with this group, and as I emerge from my tent – Willy and Brandon are already up and out – I realize today isn't going to be much better than last night. Trent is yelling at Danny for being dumb, Brandon is yelling at Trent for being a jerk, September is yelling at everyone, Jarri is back in death-metal land and yelling at nobody, and worst of all Miss Stillman is lying motionless against a log in the campfire circle. She's breathing, to be sure, but something worse than an asthma attack is clearly going on. Kate's trying to help her, but she can't juggle everything.

I'm about to try to take control when Miranda has a different idea. She's not unconscious, I realize, and might be about to turn the corner. That would be so good. I lean down next to her, so that only Kate and I can hear her.

"Pedro, I need you to stay here. Let Kate take the group and find a way to civilization. There are towns nearby. We can't be more than an hour's walk from someone who can send cops and paramedics."

"Do you think that's what you need?", asks Kate.

"No, not for me. I just need a little more rest."

"Would you mind telling us what else is happening? Asthma doesn't do this."

"No. Something's very wrong here. I feel like I've been drugged. Or poisoned. Or both."

Lily, I realize, is sitting close enough to hear. That's fine with me. Better her than Trent.

"Miss Stillman, does it feel like it's in your lungs? Like smoke inhalation, kind of?"

She nods. "You feel it too."

"It's probably hitting you worse because of the asthma, but I feel pretty weird too."

We puzzle it over. Kate suddenly turns and combs through the ashes of the fire. She looks aghast.

"Who was watching the fire last night?"

"I thought you were", I say, "but I guess there must have been some time when nobody had their eye on it. Why?"

Kate holds up a small metal canister, less than three inches long and half an inch thick. "This was in the fire. I can't tell what it is, but it's got a valve on the end. Pressurized. There's no label anywhere. Someone dropped this next to the fire. For all we know we're lucky it didn't blow up. Maybe it leaked something toxic into the smoke?"

Something still isn't adding up. "What did you mean we need paramedics, but not for you?"

Miss Stillman points over her shoulder to the tent she was supposed to sleep in. "The guy you brought back in the middle of the night."

I did what?

Then I remember. My brain is so fried from lack of sleep that I'd forgotten we found that guy out in the woods. Neither of the Stillmans slept a wink last night, so we stuck the guy in their tent.

"Danny! Give me a hand."

Danny's not used to being asked for help, so notorious is his reputation for incompetence, so it takes him a moment to register. We lean down by the pale green tent. Danny grabs the zipper and pulls it open.

There's nobody inside.

Before I can ponder the implications, September's voice comes loud and clear through the campsite.

"Fuck all of you! I hate you! I'm going to the road and I'm going to walk to town! This is so much bullshit!"

She storms off, running along the dirt road before Kate or I can intervene. Sep has a fairly short stride, but all the same she puts on distance pretty quickly. I wonder if I should go after her, or send Kate…

"Let her go. She'll end up at Mickey D's or Waffle World in an hour and have a nicer breakfast than the rest of us. It's not like we're completely cut off from civilization."

Kate's right, I hope. If Sep makes it to a town, she'll come to her senses after the third or fourth hash brown and get someone to come help us out. By daylight, the area doesn't seem nearly as threatening as it did in the dark. People do drive this road every day. We'll get the whole mess straightened out and be on our way across the Blue Ridge Mountains to Washington DC by mid-afternoon. The worst that can happen is we need to rent new vans.

Still, Mr. Kretschak hasn't turned up. I hope he isn't lying hurt in a ditch somewhere.

Kate has control of the situation. "Everyone, listen up. I'm not going to raise my voice, and I'm not going to repeat myself. Pedro's going to stay here, along with Miss Stillman and" – I look at Lily, who confirms what I'm thinking – "Lily and Danny will be staying here. Got that? Four people total. The rest of you are with me. Let's get that map…"

"What map?" asks Trent, without a hint of sarcasm.

"Isn't it in the van?"

Brandon checks. "I don't see it in here. Not in the glove compartment."

I sigh and check the vehicle. Not a sign of the map. There's not one in my tent, or the Stillman tent, or anywhere else that I see.

"Mr. Kretschak must have had both of the maps when he drove off. No matter, we'll just follow the road. It would be good if we could find the other van, since he must have left it and walked."

"But where is he?"

"I don't know, Willy. He probably stumbled into someone's backyard and is trying to get back here. Or maybe he's trying to find a tow truck to get the wrecked van to a garage. Heck, I could keep guessing all day. Not going to do us any good! Let's get this show on the road."

"Which way do we Cow?"

"Same way Sep went. We can catch up to her."

"The other way. Back the way we came. Toward the crash site. The maps have to be in the other van."

I sigh. Either direction – south – or southeast? – and higher up, or north-ish and lower down toward Seneca Rocks – has its merits. Without a map, I can't tell which way will get us to a town quicker. Either way, it can't be more than an hour or two before we're somewhere.

"We go back the way we came", I tell the group, "and try to find the van Mr. Kretschak took. Let's get going. There's not a moment to lose."

*****

September Lenore Janney storms down the dirt road, kicking a rock along. Two hours of sleep is not enough. She's never been so mad in her life. Yesterday she was excited by the adventure. Not this morning. She hates the group she came with. She hates West Virginia. She hates bugs! So many bugs! Argh! She kicks the rock extra hard, off the side of the road. She doesn't notice the taut wire lying three inches off the road surface until her foot has tripped it. The trap springs and pulls her nearly a hundred feet into the woods in a heartbeat, without a sound.

*****

We've gone down the road for forty-five minutes when something catches my eye. The unmistakable reflection of sunlight off glass is coming from the bottom of the valley to our left. I look. It's the van! It has to be...no, wait, it's a different kind of vehicle, a sport utility, but at least it's a sign of someone being out here.

"You guys see that? Let's go down there and see if we can find anyone to talk to."

Nobody voices an objection, so we walk along the road a little further until we come across what looks like a poorly maintained trail going down the hill. The SUV is maybe two-thirds of a mile away, the vegetation mostly ferns and tall grass. We'll be doing a bit of bushwhacking, but it *does* look like a trail.

Trent slips a little, catches himself, and tries to make it look like he did it on purpose. Willy trips a little on purpose and lands flat on the ground. I pull the column to a halt. All five boys roll their eyes at me, expecting a lecture.

"Stop that shit. We don't need anyone getting hurt. A twisted ankle could slow the whole group down."

"She's right", mansplains Trent, "remember how Ricky got his ankle all messed up..."

He trails off.

"Where the hell is he?"

Chase's question hangs in the air. I can't remember seeing the sophomore all morning. From Willy and Brandon and Jarri's expressions, neither can any of them. Trent starts to pace.

"Okay, he was in his tent last night, right? We saw him rolling around in his sleep. He's probably still there."

"No he's not", says Chase. "That tent was definitely empty. Danny dropped that log, right before you started yelling at him, and it rolled right across the red tent. There's nobody in there."

"Oh gosh, maybe that was *him* we were tracking last night,

not his uncle. It was his phone, after all."

I round on Jarri. "What happened last night?"

"We found that guy, up on the hill. He looked like he'd been lost in the woods for a while."

"Yeah, but what did you do with him? I never saw him."

"You didn't? Back me up here, Brandon, Trent. We carried that guy on our shoulders all the way down the hill and put him in the Stillmans' tent, since they weren't going to be sleeping in it."

"So he's still in the campsite with them. That's why Miss Stillman thinks we should get medical help out here. Okay, makes sense." My tired brain is putting things together as slowly as everyone else's, it seems.

We keep walking down the hill as thoughts churn furiously in my mind. I hope I have the strength to see us through this trial. It's just a misunderstanding, surely. Or a miscommunication. Gods, I am so confused.

We reach the vehicle, parked along a stretch of long grass that seems to be a very rudimentary track. It's facing uphill toward the road we've come off of. Blue-gray, a functional if not particularly stylish American brand. Four-door, with Virginia plates.

"I guess we're pretty close to the state line, aren't we?"

I nod in reply to Trent. "Sep might be across it already."

Then Willy does what I might have expected Danny to do, if we hadn't left him at the campsite with his older sister. He opens the backseat door on the driver's side. It's not locked. We look inside.

"Whoa", says Willy, and it's all I can do not to drag him bodily away from the vehicle. He reaches inside and picks up something from the backseat.

"What is wrong with you? You can't just open a strange vehicle and start grabbing stuff!"

He frowns. "What do you mean, a strange vehicle?" Nobody even knows how to answer him, until he suddenly gets it. "Oh, this isn't Mr. Kretschak's van?"

Trent explodes. "Are you sure you're not Danny? God, I don't think *he's* even that dumb!"

Willy gets defensive. "Hey, you don't have to be a jerk!"

"Yeah he does", Brandon chimes in.

"Shut up, you little ditch digger. This is none of your…"

But he doesn't say "digger." Pushed over the edge, Brandon shoves the significantly taller Trent into the side of the car and throws a punch that misses by a mile. Trent is about to shove him back when I jump in the way, hoping the angry sophomore behind me will walk away. I should know better.

"I will get you in detention when we get back, Trent! What makes you say stuff like that?" Brandon's so mad his face looks as red as his eyes do without the color contacts.

Trent looks like he can't believe what he just said. "Okay, I'm sorry. I didn't mean…"

"You didn't mean to call me a [*he uses the racial slur*], you just did it by accident? Yeah right. Dumb fucking redneck!"

"Would someone mind explaining to me what is going on here?" I'm hoping we can keep moving. No good is going to come from checking out this vehicle, not with this bunch. If the owner comes back to find a door open and teenagers fighting next to his car…ugh, how much worse can this get?

"Well", says Brandon, "I think it makes perfect sense! Trent is a racist piece of white fucking trash…"

Chase, who I just now realize has been peeing on the tires on the other side of the vehicle, pipes up. "Why would he call you the n-word? It's not like you're, you know, black."

"Yeah I am. What, you didn't think black people could be

albinos? You've never seen my parents?"

I haven't, but somehow, I trust that he's telling the truth. But now I'm wondering, did Trent know?

"Check this out! It's a little canister of something. There's like a hundred of them in here."

Willy, as if nothing had happened, is actually rummaging through the contents of the vehicle. He emerges holding a small unmarked black canister with a pressurized valve, just like the one I found in the ashes of the fire. A sinking feeling pulls my stomach into a deep pit. This is unreal.

"Willy, drop it and leave it!"

"Nah, I don't think I have to do what you say. You're not a teacher. Also, Cows."

"No, I'm a person with basic common sense. Unlike you."

"I don't have to listen to you. You hit me yesterday and called me a bad word. Then you said stuff about millions of years. I don't believe in that stuff. I think I should ignore you."

Chase, doing just that to me, pulls out a lighter. "Dude, let's blow it up! I wonder what it is." He grabs the canister and shakes it.

I snatch it out of his hands. They have no idea how stupid they're all being. "Chase, enough! What *happens* if this stuff blows up? What if the other canisters blow up from that? We could all get killed. Put it back where you found it or so help me!"

"I didn't find it. Willy did."

"I'm in no mood for this. That stuff is pressurized, whatever it is! You know what that means?"

"I know what it means! If you drop it hard enough, it blows up. Did you know if you puncture an oxyacetylene welding tank, it'll fly half a mile?"

"I'm not even going to ask how you know that. Put it down."

Chase sneers at me. "Make me. I don't think you're strong enough to OWW!"

I go for the pressure points on either side of his neck.

"Who the heck is this guy?", Jarri wonders. "A couple hundred little pressurized canisters without labels. An unlocked car parked way down in the valley. Either this stuff is worthless, or they think nobody's going to come here, or...oh no."

I realize what he's thinking at the same moment.

"Someone wanted us to find this."

Jarri nods. "I think so."

"We need to get out of here now! Back to camp!"

"Why back to camp?"

"He dropped one of them in the fire last night when none of us were looking! It's some kind of poison."

Trent, his brow deeply furrowed, looks askance. "Who?"

"The driver of the vehicle. The guy you found in the woods last night. Same person. He got you to 'rescue' him so he could drop that thing into the fire. It didn't explode but maybe it was supposed to. We've got to get back and warn the others before he kills them!"

Jarri isn't sure, although he does at least follow me. "That guy seemed really desperate."

"He must have been faking it to get sympathy."

Brandon, unfortunately, overhears just enough to misunderstand what I'm talking about.

"Why should I believe you? You're as bad as Trent!"

"Brandon, that's *not* what I was saying!"

Willy shuts the vehicle door and starts walking back uphill to the road. "Let's go, then."

From where he is, Willy, like Chase and Trent, can't see what I do: the sunken footpath leading straight in the direction of the campsite, diagonal to the road. It'll be quicker than going back up to the road. I have to wonder if the place where the vehicle is parked is an unmarked trailhead. Maybe I'm reading too much into this. But I'm not going to voice any doubts now.

"This way! There's a path that goes more directly to camp."

"How do you know it goes to camp?", Trent asks, coming to where he can see it too.

"It's the right direction. Every moment we stand here talking about it is a moment that guy could be hurting people at camp. Hurry up!" I run forward without waiting. To my relief, they all follow.

We've gone maybe half a mile when the hills are starting to tower over us. The path is not going as far up as I'd expected. We're probably still two hundred feet below the level of the road. The ground beneath our feet is very stony, the ground forming two steep walls on either side. If we were in the Southwest, I'd worry about flash floods. It's like we're in a dry riverbed. Maybe we *are*.

A stone crashes down from several feet up on the left, and I come to a stop. Argh, maybe this was a mistake. We might have to climb our way up. Should I concede that I was wrong and have us go back the way we came?

Willy freezes, a deer-in-the-headlights expression plastered on his face. "Cows are coming", he states, matter-of-factly.

I ignore him. "I wish I'd brought my rope! This looks like it's going to dead-end…what's that noise?"

I can hear a rumbling sound coming from up ahead, behind a bend in the trail. Jarri, Chase, Brandon, and Trent can clearly hear it too. We look at Willy, who looks equal parts enraptured as if he's seeing an angel and horrified like he's looking straight into the bowels of Hell.

Not that *I* believe in Hell, of course, though I'm sure he does.

Willy's face is white as a sheet of paper, drained of blood even from his pasty complexion.

"Cow-OW-oo-oh-ows are com-ing!", he pronounces in a weird ululation, as if invoking some long-forgotten deity.

Unfortunately, he's right. I didn't know there were cattle ranches in West Virginia, but all of a sudden there's a herd of cows running down the ravine toward us, from the direction we're going toward. There's no time to do anything but run like hell.

It doesn't do much good. We can't outrun a stampede like this. I find a place where the side of the path isn't too steep and climb up, hauling Brandon up behind me. Jarri finds a tree on the other side of the path, while Willy manages to get up onto a boulder near him. Chase and Trent are still in the path of the stampede.

Then Chase trips and one of the front cows runs straight over him. Trent runs to his side, pushing against the oncoming cows, and yells something. Chase rolls out of the way into a ditch as Trent does the stupidest thing I've seen him do yet.

Facing a charging cow, Trent grabs onto the animal's neck, jumps, and tries to swing onto its back. He fails miserably. Unable to clear the animal's height, Trent falls straight under its hooves and screams in pain. The next cow runs him over as he lies there. And another cow, and another. The last of the cows run past and I jump down from my perch, swiftly joined by Jarri and Willy. Brandon is still sitting where he and I rode out the stampede, shaking with fright.

"Trent! Trent, are you okay?" Jarri is at Trent's side, nudging his shoulder. It doesn't look good. Trent has a huge cut on his forehead and a black eye. It looks like several hooves landed on his abdomen, and there's at least one bleeding cut on his lower torso. Deep red blood is soaking through his light tan shirt. I can't imagine the pain he must be in.

Against my judgment, Trent sits up. "It doesn't hurt as much like this", he whispers feebly, though we all can tell that it's serious. Trent the hooligan has finally met his match. He winces and tries to stand, but gasps and falls back to lying on the ground.

"Leave me", he mumbles after a little while, "go get help."

"We can't leave you here in the middle of a cow highway", Jarri argues.

"I don't think there's going to be any more cows. I don't want to try move without a stretcher. Go to town. Get paramedics."

I'm about to say that we shouldn't exhaust his strength by arguing with him when the ground starts rumbling again. No tumbling rocks this time; they've all fallen from the first stampede. It seems another herd is on its way. Something must be happening at a cattle ranch somewhere east of here. Or would it more likely be a factory farm? I don't care, either way.

"Help me move him!", I yell at Jarri and Willy. Trent's the biggest person here, but Jarri's sturdily built and between the three of us we can get Trent to higher ground. He protests as we pick him up – me holding him by the ankles, Jarri under the shoulders, Willy supporting his midsection – and moans in pain as Willy trips and nearly drops him. The cut in his stomach is actively bleeding.

I hand Trent's ankles over to Brandon as we start to reach the higher ground, realizing that Chase still isn't moving either. Shouting his name, but only once – I hate it so much in movies when a character yells another character's name fifteen times in a row in situations like this – I run over to him. Chase is in a fetal position in a small depression by the edge of the path, lying totally still. The rumbling noise gets louder.

"Give me your hand. We've got to get out of here!" I reach for his arm and try to pull him to his feet before he gets trampled further. He can't be as badly hurt as Trent, can he?

Chase springs to his feet, a bruise on his other arm but otherwise looking unharmed. "Don't touch me!", he screams.

"You're not safe here! We have to get to higher…"

"Don't touch me don't touch me don't touch me!"

To my horror, Chase runs straight toward the source of the

rumbling noise, where the cows came from. No more cows come, though. Instead a huge chunk of rock breaks off and tumbles straight into the path, right where Chase is heading. He jumps back, collides with me, flips out even more, yells something incoherent, and runs toward the rock pile, scrambling over it and disappearing from view.

"Not again!" I turn to the other four above and behind me. "Nobody else goes running off!"

"Trust me", says Trent, "I'm not going anywhere."

I climb up to the spot where Willy, Brandon, and Jarri are gathered around the injured Trent.

"That was pretty stupid, wasn't it?", Trent says through gritted teeth. He sort of laughs at himself, but it causes a fresh wave of pain. "Oww. I think I've got a broken rib."

"What the hell were you thinking?", asks Jarri. "Trying to be Legolas?"

"Yeah", Trent sheepishly admits.

"You know he had to try that scene about twenty times before he got it right. And broke two ribs in the process."

"He really broke his ribs?"

"Yep."

"Well", I say, "I think right here is safe. As long as the weather holds."

"Doesn't look too great right now", says Brandon, confirming the latest thing I'm concerned about. The sky is full of clouds. Dark clouds. We just can't seem to catch a break today.

"Okay. Willy, Jarri, stay here with Trent. Brandon, come with me."

"Why?"

"Every decision you've made has got us from bad to worse!"

"If you hadn't wanted to go check out that car..."

"Excuse me? Willy, *you* were the one who opened the freaking door!"

"Do what she says!", yells Trent.

At least one out of four is listening to me. Brandon reluctantly following, I set off in the direction Chase went. The rockslide is still stabilizing. Brandon stumbles and gets a deep scrape on his knee. He shrugs it off and clambers over the last of the rock. We both look in surprise at what the rockslide has revealed.

There's another cave entrance right here. Small, just high and wide enough for one person to squeeze through at a time, but it's clearly not just a crack in the rock. I look inside. By the dim light of my phone – I left my flashlight back at the camp, not expecting to need it during the day – it looks like there's a decent-sized space inside. Enough to take shelter if it rains.

"Let's get inside here!" I turn around and head outside, but Brandon sticks his head in and yells.

"Chase! Are you in there?"

There's no answer. This doesn't mean he's not.

Brandon and I run back to where the others are. I explain that there's a cave not far around the next bend where we could take shelter from the rain.

"We didn't have enough time or light to thoroughly explore it, but it's enough to stay dry."

The rain starts. A distant sound of thunder convinces everyone. We manage to move Trent and soon we're all in the cave.

I just hope there aren't any more unpleasant surprises waiting for us inside. Today's been tough enough.

12: HANGED MAN

Edgar blinked slowly, the dim light showing him that he was still in the cave. For a few moments, he dared to hope it was daylight filtering in from some opening high above – no easy task to get out, perhaps, but still a sign that he and his companions might yet find rescue. He quickly surmised, once his eyes adjusted, that they had found no such luck.

The light was pale and bluish-green, and seemed to be coming from the walls of the cavern itself rather than a lantern or torch. Edgar pushed himself up to his hands and knees, finding them slick with a viscous black fluid. Still wearing only his undergarment with no sign of the clothes he'd used to pull Sarah to safety, he wondered if he would be better off walking or crawling or just staying put. There was no breeze to indicate moving air, no sound of running water; nothing at all but the soft drip of tiny droplets of water falling from the ceiling.

He could see his fingers wiggling, and that at least was something. Total darkness would have left him with no option but to hold still. None of it would have been foreign to him; he'd spent many an hour in this very cave meditating upon the haunting power and beauty of darkness. But that was by choice, and with companions safe and sound a few chambers over. He couldn't imagine what had become of Obadiah and Tobias. Worse, thought Edgar miserably, was imagining Sarah's fate, with that horrible arrow wound in this dark place.

But now his own surroundings were sufficient evil to contemplate. The dim bioluminescent glow – he remembered that word, wondering if he'd ever worked it into a story – showed that he was not near the edge of any precipice. He was in a tunnel – but what tunnel? The furthest he'd gone with Tobias, there had been oil along the walls and floor; that, of course, was what it was. Some crackpots claimed that someday oil dug up from the earth would replace whale oil as the source of light and heat for the developed world.

Whale oil...that made him think of the only novel he'd finished writing so far, concerning the harrowing voyage of a whaling vessel. It wasn't a very good book, Edgar thought, but something had made him write it. He'd been only a child the first time he sailed across the sea, forever enchanted by the thought of the boundless deeps beneath the planks of the ship. It had been during that trip eastward, a boy of six, that he'd had his first visions.

"It's never just one thing", he sometimes had to tell people when they asked him his influences. To leave out the gruesome torments meted out by Dante upon the eternally damned from the repertoire of images permanently engrained in Edgar's brain would be a terrible mistake; no less of a lapse would it be for him to neglect that he understood Dante's true intention in not speculating how things might be in the afterlife but rather exposing the painful truth of how sinfully human beings lived in this world. Both in his later childhood years in Britain and as a young man in America, he'd met enough Irish people to absorb the great legends this uniquely introspective seafaring folk had built up over the years, tales of ancient voyages across an ocean that seemed to truly represent a rugged exploration of the human soul. Even the *Odyssey* of Homer, Edgar was convinced, truly told of a man's journey through his own traumatized heart and soul rather than through actual islands.

In all of those stories, Edgar often mused, it had to be those who suffered most who learned the deepest truths, the ones that could not be fully expressed in words. He had heard tales of explorers in remote corners of the Amazon and Siberia, two places he doubted he'd ever see with his own eyes, who told of holy men who believed they must first be spiritually dismembered and impaled upon a cosmic axis before they could arrive at enlightenment. No Christian did Edgar consider himself, certainly not since she who was nevermore had been taken, but he recognized in their Savior something universal of the hero suspended in the gap between earth and heaven, life and death, to do battle with the forces of spiritual evil and win truth and holiness that worldly life could not afford. Odin too, the equivalent god of the Norse, had been such a "hanged man", a cosmic shaman who could bring to humanity the wisdom of writing and good governance only after nine days hanging upon the tree at the heart of the world.

"Well", Edgar said to himself as his thoughts raced along, "I hope I shan't need to spend nine days in this living tomb. Even three would be too much. Sarah! Where can she be?"

Going in either direction seemed to do no good, yet with Sarah's life in danger, he didn't dare wait. He'd lost any sense of direction along with consciousness, but somehow one direction seemed to be slanting slightly upward and he knew he must take it. The bioluminescence didn't fade as he worked his way along, soon feeling with more certainty that the tunnel indeed led to higher ground. How many fathoms below the earth he might be, he could only wonder. Despite the autumnal cold he would have felt above the surface wearing so little, Edgar didn't even shiver. The cave, he realized, was the same temperature night or day, winter or summer.

Were he a fish in no need of air at the surface, Edgar figured, his current predicament would be no different from swimming the depths of the great ocean. The comparison seemed important to him, for some reason he couldn't put his finger on. The thought of his character Arthur Pym came back to him; why had he and his shipmates endured all the horrors, perils that even now made the misadventure of Edgar and his companions seem mild?

They were hunting whales. These folk went into one world of perilous depths looking for wealth and a source of power to bring back to their homes; how different, really, were the motivations of Edgar and Sarah and her cousins?

His brain started racing. Not once had he been able to explain why he'd written that silly book; it was as if it had written himself and he were merely the hand that turned it from disembodied word into embodied. Down here in the depths of the earth, the horrifying realization came to him. He had been chosen to write that story because he was in it now. Exchange sea for land, and he was on or near the island of Tsalal that he'd written about to entertain people who enjoyed schlocky horror.

At least that meant he had a way out of the labyrinth. How had Arthur Pym and Dirk Peters made it away from their monstrous captors? Edgar racked his memory, wishing he'd bothered to actually read the book after he finished writing it.

They'd been ambushed in a narrow gorge, just like in his book; now he was in a maze of subterranean passages, struggling to know whether they'd been carved by some kind of goblins or merely by the action of water over an unspeakably long time. Now if only he wasn't alone. It was terrible being alone.

Just when he had begun to wonder if he would ever see another human being, Edgar heard the voice. A male voice, its pitch strange and distorted, but clearly not Obadiah or Tobias. It didn't sound like a Scots accent, though, giving him hope that its owner did not hail from the murderous Clan MacGregor. He tried to make out the words the strange man was saying.

Then his blood froze as a different sound came from behind him. Someone, or something, was shuffling along the passage, having followed him. Edgar knew the light wasn't good enough to rule out having passed by some side passage along the way, somewhere a potential attacker could have come from. He wondered if he dared run. A small man like himself rarely won a fistfight, and whatever it was sounded *big*.

A hand closed around his ankle. There was nothing else for it. Edgar kicked and his bare foot found a face, a decidedly human face, hitting it in the open mouth. Teeth closed on his foot, a bestial rage erupting from his attacker. He screamed and fought back. A sudden flash of light broke out, sparks igniting some tiny pocket of gas just big enough to shed momentary light without consuming all the breathable air. In the moment before darkness fell across his vision, Edgar saw distinctly the face of Obadiah Royster, eyes bloodshot, mouth foaming, a look of utter terror and panic stamped across his face. When the light disappeared, even the bioluminescence was no match for Edgar's blinded eyes.

Obadiah screamed and grunted. Now new sounds assaulted Edgar; snarling growls, like those of a dog or other carnivorous beast, joined the sounds of tearing flesh. Obadiah ceased to move or make sound, and Edgar knew that any misgiving he'd had about the burly man had been unfounded. Tough as he was, Obadiah had met something down here that was far more dangerous than him, and now Edgar was about to meet it too.

But rather than lunge for his throat, the attacker seemed to retreat, leaving Obadiah's body behind. Edgar checked for a pulse, but the pool of warm blood and the terrible bite through the throat told him he would find none. Shivering, Edgar pulled Obadiah's shirt and pants off the corpse and dressed himself with them; even clothes that were much too loose were an improvement over no clothes.

Human footsteps approached, at least two pairs of them. The voice he'd heard minutes ago spoke, words Edgar knew were English but could not comprehend. Then the other voice spoke, and his heart sank even deeper as he recognized it.

"That's him."

"How much do you think he knows?", replied the other, intelligible at last.

"Your guess is as good as mine, uncle. We leave him here, in the dark. I'm sure he'll appreciate the touch. He could practically have written this story himself."

Now he knew who the other voice belonged to, and could not have felt more betrayed. His undoing, coming at the hands of one he'd admired so much, sickened him. Who had given him ideas for what might lie in the dark recesses of the human heart? Who had stoked his imagination with tales of the ghostly whale off the coast of Chile whom so many believed to be a supernatural messenger warning against taking too much from the earth?

Edgar cursed himself for not putting it together sooner. Of course they were related! He'd thought the name fairly common, and perhaps it was, but here they both stood, clearly kin, clearly conspiring to do to him what one of his characters had once done to another. It could not be allowed to happen.

Edgar flung himself at one of the two figures, not caring which one it was. The other kicked him and sent him sprawling, hitting his head hard upon the wall of the tunnel. He grabbed onto the first limb he could find and pulled hard, yanking the uncle down into a heap as he put all his strength into smashing the nephew's head against the wall.

"What did you do with her?!" he wailed as he vented his fury upon Tobias.

"She's fine!", protested Tobias as his uncle, the explorer Jeremiah Reynolds, pulled Edgar off him.

Jeremiah threw a punch at Edgar, who pretended to have lost consciousness again. He could feel himself being slung over the legendary explorer's back as the uncle and nephew set off on a passage Edgar could no longer sense leading up or down.

"We take him to the High Priestess", Jeremiah insisted, "leave him there. If they spare him, he'll still never find his way out of here."

Tobias seemed to have assented without speaking loud enough for Edgar to hear him, for they kept going at a good pace. Edgar felt more miserable than he'd ever felt before, and wished dearly for his home in Richmond, curled up with a cat and a cup of tea and a book totally different from the ones he wrote. Yet a feeling of deep curiosity smothered his fears. Was this not the culmination of his many years of visions in the dark? Had he not suffered as much as any man ever did, and if Christ and Odin and the shamans of distant lands spoke truthfully, should he not be reaching his reward of enlightenment?

The bioluminescence along the cavern walls grew brighter as they descended, until at last Edgar felt like he would be able to read by it. He could not imagine how far down they were now. They crossed a subterranean stream, Edgar still flopping over Jeremiah's shoulder like a sack of grain, and although there were other streams higher up in the caves, he had to wonder if this might be the one at the bottom of the gorge they had climbed across.

When they finally stopped and Jeremiah set him down, he tried to keep up the pretense of unconsciousness, but failed. It was next to impossible, he knew, to suppress the urge to catch oneself when falling. Tobias and Jeremiah glared at him, then exchanged knowing glances.

"I think you're going to like this, Edgar", said Tobias with a sinister smile that Edgar could not believe he was seeing. This was nothing like the man he'd known and befriended.

"Why?", he croaked, his voice sounding much like a raven.

"Why, Mr. Poe? Why are we leaving you here? You know too much. You're about to discover even more, things that will fulfill your wildest dreams before you die down here. I wouldn't count on that happening too soon, either. You could have quite a life down here. *They* seem to be perfectly content."

Edgar shuddered. "Tell me Sarah's alright!"

"I already did", said Tobias. "She'll be on her way to Richmond by now, ready to forget that any of this ever happened."

"More to the point", broke in Jeremiah, "it is time for you to make your final discovery. Nothing worth having ever comes without a price. A sacrifice must be made, a life surrendered to the darkness in exchange for turning the darkness into light."

Saying this, he stroked a part of the wall without any glowing algae on it, his hand coming away dripping with sticky black oil. Edgar understood. Just as the people in his novel – and in Jeremiah Reynolds' own stories from the South Pacific – had found themselves unwilling sacrifices to the cruel gods of the sea in exchange for the whale oil that kept the world lit, he was now to become the sacrifice offered to these demons of the underworld in exchange for a different kind of oil.

"You've written this story before", the elder Reynolds went on, confirming Edgar's thoughts, "and you were going to write it again, weren't you? Oh, Mr. Poe, you have such a flair for exposing the dark heart of humanity, yet so inept at escaping it yourself."

"What's down here?!", Edgar snapped, cutting off the explorer. "What am I going to find? What secret could be worth all of this? You killed Sarah already, didn't you?"

Jeremiah struck him. "I saved her from that MacGregor punk, you ungrateful buffoon!"

Tobias stepped between them. "Enough. We have an

audience to keep. Let us meet our hostess with respect."

Jeremiah nodded. "Can you walk, Poe?"

Edgar shrugged. He'd rather meet his destiny on his own two feet, as bruised as they were, to say nothing of the bite from Obadiah.

They carried along, and soon the ceiling soared high above, full of bioluminescent light. Huge stalactites hung overhead, some black silhouettes against the pale blue and others covered in the glowing algae. The floor was rough and full in places with pools of water. He stumbled only once, his foot splashing loudly in the water, but kept his balance and followed the Reynolds team.

"Tobias, please. Is there nothing you can tell me?"

"What would I need to say to you? We've descended so far into the earth, thinking only of how to exploit it and make money, that we came across the equal and opposite reaction to our race's greed. Did you think the people who live on the outside of this globe were the only human race?"

"You're saying there are folk who dwell down here?" Edgar pondered the implications and nearly cheered. He turned to Jeremiah "All this time, you were right! The earth is hollow! How many other entrances are there? Is this cavern connected to the South Pole?"

To his surprise, Jeremiah rounded on him. "I wasted the best years of my life on that stupid theory! I staked everything on getting Congress to sponsor an expedition to the inside of the earth, and now I'm a laughingstock in Washington! You know nothing, Mr. Poe. There's no other way out of here outside of Virginia."

Edgar shrugged. Even without being connected to other underworlds, the space excited him plenty. He couldn't be sure because of the hue of the light, but it looked like the water in the larger pools was strangely thick – mixed with oil, perhaps – and seemed multicolored. He'd been here before in his dreams, and written it into that silly book of his. Actually seeing it was more powerful than he had expected.

Now, he wondered, how did the story end?

Tobias and Jeremiah stopped and the latter spoke. "The road ends here, Poe. Down here, it is you who are the sacrifice and I the magician. You have followed the magician and his nephew to the altar. We need only await the presence of the High Priestess."

It seemed an eternity passed. Tobias and his uncle stood motionless over Edgar, allowing him to sit on a nearby slab of rock. They faced him and he them, so that when at last their faces betrayed something akin to fear, he could not see what they were looking at behind him. Nor did he dare turn around. He would rather not see it, he had decided. Let the beast devour him and do it quickly.

Jeremiah bowed respectfully to the unseen thing behind Edgar, Tobias following suit a split second later. Edgar froze as they backed up, walking away from him without turning around. The Reynolds pair had gone more than a hundred feet before they finally turned and walked briskly out of the cavern. He could bear it no longer as he lost sight of them, and forced himself to look over his left shoulder.

An unbelievably huge shrouded white figure loomed up at him out of the darkness. Edgar could not explain it. His brain did not even want to. He stared awestruck as it bent down over him, sniffing him and revealing itself to be a creature of flesh and blood. The light from the algae was enough for him to recognize familiar objects, but not to determine the nature of this strange being.

A chorus of low humming, almost like the purr of a great cat, broke the silence in the dim cavern all around him. The sound was coming from every direction and getting louder. Edgar spun his head from side to side, trying to get a visual on its source. Something was moving in nearly every part of his horizontal vision.

As they drew closer, he could recognize forms, human-like but with the heads of beasts like wolves or dogs, slinking toward him. Some went bipedal, others crawling on all fours. The huge figure above him, while covered in a white shroud, seemed like it might be of the same sort. He could distinguish two firm feet on the ground, like those of a man but with much more hair, and a pair of arms, and a terrible long snout for a face. It was hidden, like almost all of the mysterious creature's flesh, but as the folds of the shroud moved, he could make out the outline of sharp teeth in its mouth, and claws on its hands. It made not a sound as it pointed to him.

Edgar woke up, knowing it had to have been a dream. Things like this didn't happen in reality. It was just another vision, giving him an idea of what to write about next. But something was terribly wrong. He was still in the cave. Still wearing clothes that were much too big for him. All the blood was rushing to his head. Somehow, he was upside-down. His ankles hurt unbelievably. A trickle of white foam leaked from his mouth as he felt the desire to run wild on a moonless night, snarling and biting.

He was trapped in a very narrow place, his legs wedged so tightly he could not see through the shaft they were in and confirm, as he suspected, that he had been hanged by a rope around his ankles. Exerting all the strength in his abdominal muscles, Edgar pulled his torso upward to a perpendicular angle with his legs – and gravity – so that at least the pressure was no longer all on his head. He could not remember how he'd come to be here. How much of what he'd just experienced had been real?

That Tobias had turned on him out of greed, he had no doubt. That Obadiah was dead, he could also not question. Sarah's fate remained a mystery. As for the cave creatures – they must have been his imagination, surely. He wiggled his way downward until his legs came free of the tight passage, although the rope held. And a good thing, too; with his body out of the passage, he now saw that he'd been in a ventilation shaft, dangling high above the floor in one of the upper passages. He swung a bit, keeping his eyes on the ceiling, and suddenly the image of a leering skull bore down upon him from on high.

He'd seen it before. He could find a way out. Back to the land of the living it would be for him. He reached up to his ankles, and on the way his hand caught a strip of a white shroud tied around his waist. It was too recognizable to be a coincidence. Everything down there had been real. He could no longer control his reaction. Hanging upside down in the cavern, he laughed like a maniac until he had worn out the last ounce of his strength and could laugh no more.

He'd looked into the heart of darkness and lived to tell it.

13: DEATH

Pedro and Danny race along, no longer able to wait for Kate's group to find help, hoping we did the right thing by leaving Lily and Miranda at the campsite. There's no trace of the battered man Jarri and Trent and Brandon and I found last night. No trace of Ricky either. Yet something was moving in the Kretschaks' tent last night, people have agreed, and if it wasn't Ricky, I can't begin to imagine what it was.

We have to reach the outside world now. The trail we took with Mr. Kretschak yesterday afternoon has to lead somewhere, probably into someone's backyard. Sooner or later, there will be a house, a church, a restaurant, *something*. We may be in a wild and wonderful state, but it's not an unoccupied one. How far can we possibly be from civilization?

"We're almost at the cave", Danny says, remembering yesterday's adventure. "This is where Sep was standing when Ricky kicked that rock and we found the cave!"

"So?", I ask as I keep running. "It doesn't matter."

But no sooner are the words out of my mouth than something does matter. I know the second I see her that she's dead.

Danny gasps and runs to September's side. Checks for a pulse at her throat. Does it wrong. I check correctly. Same response. Nothing. Her eyes stare blankly at the sky. There's no expression on her face. No blood anywhere. No sign of life at all.

We're paralyzed with horror. This isn't some prank. She's not going to suddenly sit up and yell "boo!" at us. This time, we really have fallen into a horror movie. Our classmate is dead. I look at Danny, and he looks at me. In that instant, I know that no matter what disagreements we may have, no matter how I may have got on his case before, Danny and I are permanently joined by this.

At least he's not Willy.

I've seen death before, plenty of times, but never here in

America. Here, I thought people were safe. Here, I thought, they don't just die young for no reason. I was so wrong.

"She was only sixteen", Danny gasps. "She can't be dead, she can't be!" He looks like he's going to vomit. I pull him away from her corpse. He crumples into a sobbing heap as I try to check her over. There's not a mark on her body. I'd be able to tell if she died in a struggle, but her face shows me that she never saw it coming, whatever it was. Something killed her quickly.

No, I realize, I was wrong about one thing. There is a mark. Rope burn around both of her ankles, as if someone tied her up. Yet the killer didn't drag her, or there'd be more marks…nope, there they are, on her hands, as if she had instinctively braced herself against a fall. Sighing, I give up trying to examine the body. I'm not a coroner. I'm probably going about this completely wrong.

But I have to know what happened to her. Why would someone kill her? What did this harmless young girl ever do to anyone? I feel like it must have been a terrible, tragic accident.

Danny's sobbing uncontrollably, looking as much disgusted as sad. He's dry-heaving, collapsed face-down on the ground in front of the cave entrance. I try to pull him to his feet.

"This is all my fault!", he bawls. "I killed her! It's my fault she died." I wait for him to explain. "I threw that stone yesterday. Knocked it into the cave. I woke up something down there, didn't I? One of the invisible ghosts. It killed her. It should have been me!"

Normally, I'd round on him for having done something so irresponsible, but it doesn't seem right in front of Sep's body.

"Why her? Why did they kill her and not me? I'm as bad as them. I never treated her like a person. All I saw was her body. Now that's all that's left of her. I treated her like an object. That's no different from killing her, is it?" He breaks down, incoherent.

I don't know what to say. The image of September swatting away at her chest, at the ice cube Danny slipped between her breasts, comes unbidden to my mind. There's something unspeakably awful about the harsh contrast between Sep as she was in life, vivacious and flirtatious and full of silly exuberance, and the awful crushing reality of her lying here dead in front of us. Somehow, I know she didn't mind the incident with the ice cube. I suspected, prior to this trip, that Sep was only coming along in the hopes of losing her virginity to one of the boys. Ricky, perhaps? Girls drool over him in the hallway. It would be a mistake to think only guys have sexual urges or objectify the opposite sex, although Berghall teachers seem to make that mistake in general. Sep did plenty of it. She was no different from Danny; just a kid, hormonal and repressed and looking to have a bit of fun. She deserved better than this, even if she'd done nothing with her life so far. The memory of every kid I ever saw die in Afghanistan flashes past my eyes once in a while. Now Sep joins the ghastly parade.

"We should at least cover her up", I say futilely, looking for a suitable shroud. "But we have to get moving. Who's going to be next if we don't find help? Lily? Your sister?"

"Ricky", Danny says. "I bet he's dead too."

"We don't know that. We do know more bad things are going to happen unless we get to civilization soon."

Kate is thinking the same thing as the sound of thunder rolls across the valley outside. We're inside the cave, far enough from the entrance to stay dry but not too far back. Jarri has a flashlight, the only one of us to have thought of grabbing on one this daylight mission, and it looks like the cave goes back a *long* ways.

"I'm going to die", Trent croaks feebly.

"No you're not", says Jarri. "We're going to get out of here and get you to a hospital."

I check over Trent. He's not actively bleeding anymore, but he's not looking too good either. I give him a decent sip of water, out of the only bottle we have along. Yet another area in which we were unprepared. We thought by now we'd be at a sheriff's office trying to find Mr. Kretschak. Instead we're in this cave and no closer to figuring out what happened to our teacher than we ever were.

"Jarri, can I have your flashlight?"

"Sure. Here, take it. I hope it's got a longer battery life than the GPS did."

By my watch, it's well into the afternoon already. How did the day go so fast? We were supposed to be into the DC area by now. I start to think maybe the DC leg of the trip – seeing the US Capitol, the Smithsonian, the war and presidential memorials – isn't going to happen at all unless we get rescued quickly.

Jarri, crouching over Trent, keeps talking to him. I don't follow what he's saying, but to the minimal extent that I can read people's auras, Trent seems calmer. Willy's curled up in a nook some distance away, asleep. Brandon looks like he's meditating. I decide to take a look further back by myself, but not get too far away. Surely Chase ran into the cave earlier. He's got to be back here somewhere.

Away from the sounds of the thunderstorm outside, I hear a new noise from within the cave. Running water. There's an underground stream somewhere close. I shine my light around and find it. It's flowing from left to right, a few feet wide and about one deep. The other side looks like a wide area with a flat floor, but what catches my mind is the piece of wood lying on the far bank. It looks like it was supposed to be mounted on a post but fell down a long time ago. There's writing on it, carved and painted. One word, or name, that I can't make heads or tails of. It looks like…Finnish.

I fetch Jarri, discovering that Trent has fallen asleep. We can leave him for a moment. Jarri follows me back to the stream.

"Look over there. Is that a word that means anything to you, on that sign?"

He shudders and takes a step back. "Tuonela. The underworld. A land of eternal shadows where the dead dwell. No living person except a great shaman may cross the river of the dead."

So now we've discovered a river separating the land of the living from the land of the dead. Today just keeps getting better and better.

14: ALCHEMIST

September 2007
Berghall Academy, Covington, Kentucky

"You know what would make a great game? Have a spinner or a computer program that randomly chooses an element for each player in turn, and whatever element you get, you have to put a little block of it into a test tube. Whoever's blows up last wins."

Everybody laughs, even the teachers. I don't know this Willy Cunningham kid too well, but he's got a good sense of humor. **Pedro** and ten other students are sitting around the geology classroom after school, holding a pre-trip meeting. I'm excited to go on this trip next month during fall break. It will be nice to see some nature and some cultural sites I haven't yet experienced, and it'll be nice to get to know these younger students.

Danny, I know, is Miss Stillman's younger brother, while Ricky is the nephew of this Mr. Kretschak and the son of the other one. The school has never, in the four years that I've attended it, resolved the issue of how to distinguish between the brothers who both teach here. Anyway, Danny and Ricky seem like pretty close friends, and I've definitely seen them and Willy, and Trent, and a bunch of other guys who are like them, out in the field during lunch playing a different "last one standing" game. They spin around and around to get dizzy, then run around and crash into each other, so it's literally the last one standing who wins. Dizzy fights, I think they call it. They're not a sophisticated bunch, but they know how to have fun.

"Okay", says Mr. Kretschak, "back to business. Jackson, talk to me after the meeting about your friend. After that business in Mrs. Hutton's class today, I'm not sure he should come, but you're free to try convince me. Who else do we have. Suriah Greitang?"

She raises her hand. "I go by Lily."

"Oh, okay. So why are you interested in the trip?"

"I've never been in a cave. Will we go pretty far inside any? It sounds so cool."

"Well, I don't know how it'll compare to what you've heard, but we will be poking around in a few small caves near Seneca Rocks. Not the kind that you go all the way in and get total darkness, I wish we had the resources to do that, but if you want that you should go to Mammoth sometime. Who all's been there?"

Several hands go up – we are in Kentucky, after all – but not quite all. That one girl with all the makeup shakes her head no. What was her name, again? September, I think. Her parents must be weird. I've been to Mammoth, just once, possibly the furthest I've been from Cincinnati within the United States. After they recovered me from the streets of Afghanistan, my only remaining possession the canteen, my parents had little desire to travel. They picked a city, got jobs at a local insurance firm, and tried to jump into suburban American life as if they'd been living it all along. I need only look at my classmates to see how I would have turned out if this life were the only one I'd ever known.

"We'll get to see a really good cross-section of Appalachian geology, at any rate", Mr. Kretschak continues, "so if you want to get up close with rocks and waterfalls, you've come to the right place."

Miss Stillman puts in her two cents. "But if you're more interested in the social sciences, we have plenty of that coming up *too*", she says with a wink toward Mr. Kretschak. "It's not going to be all rocks and stuff. We'll see the Smithsonian Museums…"

"…such as Natural History…"

"and American History, and Air and Space, on the last two days that we're in Washington. We'll be up on top of the Washington Monument on Wednesday, the first full day we'll be in DC. The whole rest of the day to stroll the Mall and take pictures next to monuments. That, I'm guessing, is what you're more interested in."

She directs her attention to September, who shrugs. "Maybe. I've never been out of, like, the tri-state area before, so I'm just really, like, excited to see all these, like, places that I've heard of. Will we get to do any spelunking while we're in West Virginia?"

My secret crush, Kate, snickers and tries to make it look like a cough. Mr. Kretschak just looks confused. Miss Stillman answers.

"Lily asked that question already, September. We'll be checking out some small caves near Seneca Rocks."

"Yeah, but I was asking about spelunking."

I can't help it. "What do you think spelunking means?"

"I don't know what it means, I just thought it sounded cool."

"Spelunking", says Mr. Kretschak without any condescension, "means exploring a cave. From the Latin *spelunca*, meaning cave."

September looks like she just watched a movie scene with a huge twist. "OHH! I get it now."

"I can only speak for myself", says Lily, "but I'm really fascinated about caves. I spend a lot of time on artsy websites and read a lot of folklore. There are caves all over the world where there's supposed to be people living who can only be seen if you're willing to believe in them."

Jarri, the headphone-wearing Finnish kid whose only communication earlier in this meeting was to nod when his name was called, perks up. "I'm not the only one who believes in them! Yay!"

Lily laughs nervously. "I'm not sure 'believe' is the word I'd use, but yeah, I kinda hope to see one someday."

"We should try see if we can sneak off and find one!"

Jarri's a little too enthusiastic. I picture Lily, slight and slim and prim and proper, alone in a cave with Jarri the unruly caveman, and I don't like the image. Neither does she, it seems.

"Nobody's going to go sneaking off", says Mr. Kretschak. "People get lost in the woods every year in that part of the state because they go hiking without maps. About five years ago, a geologist I used to see at conferences actually disappeared exploring a cave in another part of West Virginia. He went in too far without adequate supplies and got lost."

"Did they find him?", I find myself asking.

"No."

The group gets weirdly silent for a second.

"But that's not anywhere near where we're going. You guys will be perfectly safe as long as you follow directions and nobody sneaks off. Also:

"Jack and Jill went up the hill,
to fetch a pail of water;
there they stayed, and there they played,
and now they have a daughter."

He sings this, eliciting nervous giggles from around the table.

"Yeah, that happened the first year we did this trip. What a mess. Almost got the trip shut down for the future. So none of that, mm-kay?"

"Who were the people...?", Trent begins to ask. Miss Stillman shushes him.

"Never mind that. What he's saying is, it doesn't happen this year. We will have a strict curfew where you have to be in your *own* tent or hotel room."

Right, I think, because I was totally planning on my high school fall break trip to West Virginia and Washington DC being a college spring break in Florida.

"I want to go back to what you were saying a minute ago, though, Lily. What should we make of legends of people living in caves? They show up all over the world. Is it just coincidence, or could there be some basis in truth?"

That's what we all love about Mr. Kretschak. He's so supportive of ideas that we come up with, even if they seem far-fetched. He says he likes to see the divine light in everyone. At an ultra-traditional Christian school, that can be a dangerous thing to say, but we students know here's one teacher we can count on.

"Well", says Lily, "on Sumatra, where my parents grew up, there are legends of little people called Orang Pendek who live in caves out in the woods, up in the mountains. A few years ago, they found fossils of little people on another island, Flores, that they're calling hobbits. Couldn't they have lived on Sumatra too? Science tells us they were definitely still around in 10,000 BC. That's recent enough that mythology could form around them."

"Same with Neanderthals in Europe", says Jarri. "There were other groups of people who moved in after the glaciers retreated, before modern humans. They left traces of their genes in our species. We learned about this in my old school in Finland when I was eleven or twelve. My teacher was pretty sure that everywhere you get legends of elves, dwarves, leprechauns, creatures like that – it's all folk memories of the original inhabitants. They had to go underground to survive once we showed up."

Miss Stillman nods, thoughtfully. "I spent a semester in Dublin in college where they had us read a lot of stuff on faerie folk. Many people in Ireland believe, even today, that the original people of the island moved underground when the first true humans showed up. The Tuatha de Danaan is what they're called. They're supposed to live in underground cities wherever there are circles of stone and barrow graves. Some people think they were a human race slightly different from us, and they took to living in caves for safety."

Willy Cunningham shakes his head. "But doesn't the Bible say all that stuff is a lie?"

Mr. Kretschak sighs. "Willy, if it were that simple, my class would be a waste of time. Berghall Academy does *not* teach young-earth creationism, and for good reason."

Willy looks surly and confrontational. I begin to rethink my first judgment of this kid. I bet he thinks the class *is* a waste of time.

"If you want to bring the Bible into this", continues Mr.

Kretschak, "look at Genesis 6:4. 'The Nephilim were on the earth in those days, and afterward, when the sons of God went down to the daughters of men and had children with them. They were the heroes of old, great warriors of renown.' Have any of you *ever* heard a pastor preach about that? Anybody's Sunday School teacher ever brave enough to deal with that verse?

"That's because nobody can prove what it's about. Some say it's accounting for the mythologies of other cultures the Judeans were in contact with when Genesis was finally written down during the Babylonian captivity. An answer to Greek myths about Zeus and other Gods fathering children. Others are convinced that a modern hermeneutic can explain it, and they're just angels. But what's an angel? The Greek word just means 'messenger'. Anything, anyone, who carries a message is an angel. Cell phones are angels. So that leaves us without much of an answer.

"Other people believe that parts of Genesis are much, *much* older than the text itself, and preserve distant memories of life in the Stone Age. So the sons of God could be modern humans, the daughters of men Neanderthals or other races similar to us. They're technically the same species as modern humans, since they were capable of having children together. The latest research suggests it was mostly modern human men and Neanderthal women."

"Wait", says Trent, "so that means some of us in this room could be part Neanderthal?"

"Like Jarri?", asks Ricky.

Jarri flips him off with his ring finger. We laugh.

"Really, if anyone's part Neanderthal today, then everyone is. You don't have to go back that many centuries to find common ancestors for basically everyone in the world."

We let that sink in. I never knew that, somehow.

"So", says Kate, unpacking the implications, "it doesn't matter if you have a bit of DNA from someone who lived that long ago, since everyone else does too, but what about dominant and recessive genes? Some people could carry certain traits that they inherit from extinct kinds of humans, that other people are also descended from but just didn't get the same specific gene?"

Mr. Kretschak looks impressed. "I never really thought about that. Wow! This is why I love having conversations that can just go in any direction they feel like. You get more interested stuff here than in most classes."

Willy looks put out. "I don't know if I want to go on this trip if you guys believe bad stuff like that."

Mr. Kretschak sighs. "Nobody's making you come along, Cunningham. You do have to learn the right science if you want to pass my class, though. No more writing 'I don't believe this crap' on quizzes about geologic eras, okay?"

"I believe what I believe, okay? Cows!"

"Believe what you want, but you need to show appropriate respect for my class. I don't want to get into this now." He turns to the rest of the group. "You know, my spiritual life has really grown since I came to understand evolutionary creationism. There's something really sacred about the fabric of the universe giving rise to the earth, giving rise to water, giving rise to oxygen, giving rise to that creative spark of *life*! I have to think of God as an alchemist using the whole universe as a grand experiment. Earth is enough of an experiment. Heck, human beings are enough of an experiment. The whole story of the Bible seems to be God wondering what's going to happen if he mixes these ingredients together and triggers this reaction or that. Sometimes, it all blows up. Not too different from that game you suggested a few minutes ago, Willy."

I love having conversations with Mr. Kretschak! It's too bad I never took a class from him. Since I took astronomy, I don't need geology for a science requirement, and I'm not going to have room to squeeze it into the spring semester. All the more reason to go on this trip next month. I think we'll have some amazing deep conversations around campfires and in DC parks.

The meeting adjourned, I follow Mr. Kretschak down the

hallway without really meaning to. Willy has slunk off in the other direction. Mr. Kretschak seems relieved.

"So, Pedro, I know I've heard about you in the school newspaper and stuff like that, but I feel like I've never really met you before."

"I would agree."

"You introduced yourself to the group as Pedro Alvarez, but according to the sheet they gave me, your last name is…"

"Alvarez Gushvenbaych. You can understand why I just go by Alvarez."

"Gushvenbaych. That doesn't sound Español."

"It's not. My mother's family are from Siberia. Her dad was the only person from their entire ethnic group to become a prominent Communist Party official. He defected in the late fifties, along with my grandmother, and they ended up in the Russian neighborhood of New York City even though they weren't ethnic Russians. They were Evenks. My mom and her brother and sister might have been the first three Evenks born in the United States."

Mr. Kretschak surprises me by actually knowing the name "Evenk". Not many people have heard of my mother's folk, who number fewer than a hundred thousand and live almost all in Siberia or northeastern China.

"So I'm half tropics, half taiga. Half fire, half ice. The only thing that runs in both sides of my family is mysticism. Dad's family have been brujos for generations, Mom's family used to be shamans. No idea what that makes me."

Mr. Kretschak chuckles. "If family occupations made you what you are, I'd be a pile of money. Long line of bankers and sleazy insurance people. My brother and I both took one look at family history and decided we wanted nothing to do with it."

I don't mention that both of my parents work for an insurance company. It's not who they are, it's just what they do for a living. Even they think it's a disgrace that the local baseball team, the one whose name my Soviet-defector grandpa always laughed at, plays in a stadium named after the company. Even the Soviets named things after people instead of after companies.

"Oh, great. Speaking of silly experiments gone wrong..."

Mr. Kretschak's voice trails off as he looks down the hallway. Trent is approaching with his emo friend in tow.

"Yeah, I have to talk with Trent and his lost puppy there about something. You wouldn't believe what those little maggots were doing in Mrs. Hutton's class this morning."

I don't want to know, and walk away with a nod of understanding. Before I've gone ten feet, I can hear Chase, the spaz who squirts people in the hallways with hand sanitizer cartridges that he's stolen from classrooms, yelling at Mr. Kretschak.

"Fuck off! I hate you! Piece of shit!"

I walk away. That's one kid I'm glad isn't going on this trip.

Mr. Kretschak is trying to find the right words as the other Mr. Kretschak, the one I was hoping to keep out of this, emerges from the nearest classroom.

"Would you care to tell me what this is about, Thomas?"

He uses my first name in front of the students. I hate it when he does that. I'd get a reprimand if I did that to a colleague.

"I guess I might as well send them your way for detention. I was just telling Alvarez over there, you wouldn't believe what they were doing in Mrs. Hutton's class when I subbed this morning."

"That's not exactly what you said!", yells Chase.

My brother looks at them, then at me, and beckons me toward the nearby empty classroom.

"Dear brother, I think we need to have a little chat."

15: DEVIL

We stand by the underground river for several minutes, not saying a word. **Jarri** doesn't know Kate well enough, but I almost feel like she believes me. We're not in West Virginia anymore, or in America at all. We've come to a place outside of the world itself. Across this small dark river is Tuonela, the land where my people traditionally believe the dead live.

"We can't cross that", I tell her, my voice hoarse. "You have to pay the ferryman to get across, if you want any chance of coming back alive. Only a trained shaman can fool the guards."

"That sounds like what the ancient Greeks believed."

"Same reality, different names for it. Their Hades, our Tuonela, Sheol for the Hebrews, it's all the same thing and we're looking at it."

Kate doesn't say anything for a while, but looks deep in thought. "Maybe I should turn off the flashlight, if we're just going to stand here. Want to save the battery for walking around."

She does, and I expect total darkness. Instead, there's still just enough faint light from the entrance we came through, now more than fifty feet up and five hundred away, to see the vaguest outlines of each other and the walls and ceiling of the cave.

"Mrs. Abischer told us last year in ancient history that the Greeks got that from Egypt. Egyptians lived only on the east bank of the Nile until fairly late in their history, because the west bank was where the sun set and the dead lived. So the border between the world of the living and the world of the dead was a river."

I ponder her words. Might my people also have imported their mythology from faraway Egypt? But if so, why are we standing on the banks of a river where the other side is actually marked "Tuonela", especially when I saw korsikko markings on the trees around our campsite to indicate the boundary between life and death was close? What else could be the explanation?

"So are you saying mythology is just made up from history?"

"There's no 'just' anything, Jarri. The Norse believed the Aesir Gods lived in a splendid city with golden domes and vast orchards within the walls. Historians have realized that the descriptions of Asgard in the old sagas are probably describing Byzantium, where enough Vikings traveled to bring back stories. Does that make their faith in their Gods, their Heaven, any less authentic just because it was based on a place on earth?"

I think about it, but other concerns win out.

"Kate, I'm not comfortable crossing that river. We should go back to the others. The storm can't last much longer."

"What are you afraid of, Jarri?"

"I'm not."

"Not what I meant. What do you fear? What would make you afraid?"

"People seeing through me. Catching the most vulnerable part of me and taking advantage of it."

"What do you mean?"

I don't play along with her game. "Why do you ask? It's an odd question."

"Because I think we've been brought here to face our fears. Here we are, in the dark, at the edge of the world of the dead. Nowhere to hide behind our pretensions and the things we fill our lives with. Here's where we have to stop hiding from the truth and confront our reality."

I don't like the sound of that. Does she know? How could she possibly know…

"The reality I see is that we've come as far as we can and should get out of here. If you want to go deeper, I won't stop you, but I feel like I'm basically killing you if I let you cross that river."

"I'm not crossing the river of the dead. I plan to sit by it."

"Wait, you believe me? I thought you Christians didn't believe that kind of thing."

"What do you mean, you Christians? I only go to this school because my parents make me."

I don't know what to say. Other than the Cutlers, I don't have parents who make me do anything. But I'm encouraged to learn that I'm not the only kid at school who doesn't fit in religiously.

"I think you and I take our faith from the same part of the world. I mean, I know Finnish isn't Indo-European, but it sounds like you've got at least some elements in common. Do you guys have an *axis mundi*?"

I know the Latin term. Yes, we share the idea with the Norse of a tree holding up the heavens, although (at least the way my grandfather told to me) ours doesn't have different worlds nestled in its branches. I nod, knowing that Kate can see it.

"Speaking as a Norse heathen myself, I don't quite share the belief in a river between life and death, but it's not far off. What you call Tuonela, I call Niflheim. We believe that caves are places where people can walk into the inside of Yggdrasil, the World Tree, and rivers within them are cross-sections of the great wells that run up and down the trunk like xylem and phloem tubes."

"So you'd agree that we're in a place where only shamans are supposed to go."

"Doesn't that make us shamans? As long as we don't get lost and as long as we get out alive."

"So far, we haven't made it out at all, and if what we are isn't lost, I don't know why that word even exists."

"What better place to be in if you're looking for enlightenment? Up against your worst fears, the deep darkness, the isolation, but no distractions, no stimulation. I feel like I could sit here forever and let go of everything."

"I don't want to hear you talking like that, Kate. This doesn't even sound like you. Aren't you the one who's always pushing us to be more responsible?"

In the dim light, I can almost see her grinning at me like she's stopped caring about everything she's been hounding the rest of us about for the past couple of days.

"Guys! Are you back there? Help!"

It sounds like Brandon. Kate snaps out of her reverie and flicks the flashlight on, and we run back the way we came, as quickly as we can without tripping or crashing into anything. Brandon is toward the back of the entrance room – the side closest to us, that is – half sitting, half lying, clutching at his right knee.

"I started to run in the dark, and tripped. Should have been more careful."

"Why did you run…where's Trent?"

Kate shines the light all around, but there's no sign of Trent.

"What the hell, Brandon? Where did he go?"

"I don't know!! I closed my eyes for a few minutes, and when I opened them, he was just gone!"

"Willy! Chase!"

Willy materializes out of the dark. At least we haven't lost him. Chase, that little punk. I'm going to kill him, unless he's managed to move Trent to a safer place.

"Okay look, Trent didn't just get up and walk away. He can't even stand. He's got to still be in the cave somewhere."

We've only got one flashlight, and who knows how long its battery will last? Gods be good, what are we supposed to do?

Pedro is thinking the same thing, other than the number of deities invoked. Nothing we do can save September. We're in worse danger here than I had any idea. Someone who wishes us harm is close by, I can sense it. There's no way Sep's death was an accident.

"Danny, keep your eyes peeled. We're not alone out here."

His face almost bloodless and covered by a waterfall of tears, Danny nods. He looks like he's aged several years today. There's a deep crinkle in his forehead, rather like one I've noticed his sister has whenever she gets flustered.

"It should have been me. Not her."

"Snap out of it! It's *going* to be us and your sister next if we aren't careful!"

But I'm torn. Do we go forward and try to find help, but risk the killer attacking the campsite? Do we go back to the campsite and make sure people there are okay? No…what good would it do to come back and tell them that September's dead, if they are okay?

"We have to keep going. Anyone we see, we watch and figure out what they're doing before we make contact."

Danny nods. "And if they're trying to kill us?"

I pick up a rock.

He gulps. "Just to defend ourselves."

"Right. Of course."

We climb further up the hill. I'm expecting the other side will greet us with a road or a house down below, but it looks like it's just more woods. The view is gorgeous, a little glimpse of rolling hills in the distance visible over the tops of the trees lower on this slope, while so much of what we can see is the forest itself surrounding us with thick dark tree trunks and blazing red-orange foliage.

This would be so perfect *if* we didn't have one person dead and another two missing. I try to enjoy the view for a second, even as I'm desperately trying to figure out which way we should go. Maybe turn left and go along the top of the hill. For all I know, there might be a better vantage point just a few hundred feet away from which I could see some building. I'm sure there are plenty of people, and homes and gas stations and convenience stores and churches, not far from here. I just wish I knew which way to get to them.

Danny nudges me. "There's somebody over there."

He nods slightly to the right, having the sense not to point. I look in what I realize must be the direction of the road we originally took from Seneca Rocks. Wherever that road is, there's a lot of hill between here and there. But there is indeed a person.

It's a man, slight of build and long of hair and beard. He's wearing tattered clothes and running in roughly the same direction we're going, about a hundred feet away. He trips once and rapidly picks himself up. I can't tell, but it almost looks like the same guy who we brought back to camp last night. Whether we should try to contact him becomes a moot point. He's seen us.

"Get out of here!", he yells. "The Dark Heart of the Raven is awake!"

Before either of us can say a word, the hobo runs down the hill, too fast to be safe. He trips again and doesn't get up. Running closer along the hilltop, I see him roll over a couple times as he falls down the hill, unable to stop. Then he's gone.

"Danny! Get over here!"

He doesn't hesitate to follow me. We make our way down to where the guy disappeared, as fast as we can without risking tripping and falling. It's a steep hill. There's no sign of the guy anywhere. No noise except a little bit of birdsong.

The ground here is covered with dead leaves, so deep that I imagine many years worth must be lying here. Nothing disturbs this part of the forest regularly enough to stir up the leaves. They lie here, disguising the more subtle elements of the topography, like the little dip in which I step and almost twist my ankle. Danny takes note and avoids that spot. He's starting to seem smarter than usual.

"Right there."

He points; I look. There's a depression in the layer of leaves, which we realize upon a closer look is not just a low patch in the ground but an absence of ground. We've found another cave opening. It's maybe three by three feet, a hole small enough I'd hesitate to try crawling inside but big enough someone could fall down it. Dreading the thought of finding another dead body, I crawl to the edge and look down.

The daylight is swallowed up in blackness long before it reaches the floor. Whether that guy's down there, Danny and I can't possibly tell. I decide to risk a "Hello!" that doesn't even echo from the well-like shaft. There's no reply.

Not that all is silence, however. There's a low rumbling coming from somewhere off in the woods, in the direction of the road. It sounds like it's a few miles away, but even from here I can tell it's not a mechanical sound. More like a rockslide, or…livestock stampeding. Another rumbling comes from the sky.

"Great. A thunderstorm at a time like this. Where should we go, boss?"

"I don't know. What do you think?"

"Pedro, I'm an idiot. Your judgment's better than mine."

"It's done us no good so far."

"Still. Anyone's judgment is better than mine. You realize it was me that threw the rock yesterday, right?"

I sigh. No sense in pointing out that he already told me that.

"Doesn't matter. Nobody died because of that. Let's go that way [I point to the left of our original direction], it looks like the highest part of the hill is up there."

We get up to a point where there's no more slope upward in any direction. It's not the exposed top of a hill, though; the entire ridge, it seems, is covered in trees. We'd have to climb a tree to see out of the forest, which doesn't strike me as a bright idea with a thunderstorm coming. However, I can try one other thing.

Hoping for a signal, I try dialing 9-1-1. There's been a fatality and now three people are missing. Unbelievably, there's still no signal. The error message tone blasts into my ear, followed by the insistent robotic voice telling me that only emergency calls are allowed here.

"This *is* an emergency call!", I yell, feeling a raging wash of déjà vu as I throw the phone down the hill into the next valley. The sound of glass breaking alerts me. Danny notices it too, and we again try to investigate. A short climb down the hill into a thick patch of trees finds us among a large pile of glass bottles, covered in grime and dead leaves.

"Some hillbilly's secret drinking spot?", Danny supposes, holding up a bottle.

"Not quite", I realize, "it's a still. Look, there's a couple of tanks. Someone was making moonshine up here. A long time ago, from the looks of it."

Danny sets down the bottle he picked up. It doesn't do what either of us would have expected it to do. Rather than rolling down the slope or just landing, it disappears from sight. Shooting me a confused look, Danny flinches. I'm as surprised as he is.

Another peal of thunder booms, louder than what we heard earlier. I duck around gnarled old tree that part of the still was probably leaning against, and there in front of me is yet another cave entrance. There's an ancient, yellowed scrap of paper inside a broken bottle just inside the mouth of this cave. Fingers trembling, I pick it up and try to read it.

"What's it say?", asks Danny, gently sliding down to the level where I'm standing.

"It's almost all rubbed out. All I can see is the last name 'MacGregor' – does that mean anything to you?"

He shakes his head.

I wish Kate were here. She did some research on this region of West Virginia and its history. Maybe she came across the name

"MacGregor" in some record of nineteenth-century settlers here. I guess it doesn't matter that much.

There's more thunder. It starts to rain. Within three minutes it's a torrential downpour. I'm surprised by how quickly it gets this intense. Picking up my phone to use its faint light, I shrug and climb into the dark space. At least it'll be dry inside the cave. Danny follows, likewise already soaked to the bone.

We sit there for over forty-five minutes as the rain doesn't let up. I'm seething. By now I could have made it to a gas station and got help. What's a little rain? I've been through much worse things than rain. Yet here I sit, hunched inside a small cave, wasting valuable time. How many more people are in danger now because I took cover instead of pressing on?

"This rain isn't going to let up", says Danny, and I feel like he's right. Kicking myself, wishing I'd decided to do this earlier, I wonder if we should try going further into the cave. I suggest this to Danny. He shrugs.

"It's probably no worse than going out there. Like, it might connect to the other cave."

"My thoughts exactly. I can't get over this feeling that we'll find something in the cave that might help us."

We set off into the darkness, using the dim light from my phone screen. The cave is really a long tunnel, boring its way into the hill. For a long time we go straight ahead, then slowly curving left, then sloping down. There aren't any big precipices or huge stalactites that I can see. Just a long passage, heading down and down.

But it's not empty. Danny and I notice surprising things – rotting wooden furniture, a smashed chest full of clothes, a rusty set of pots and pans – lying in the tunnel every so often. Clearly the cave has been used. Lived in, it looks like. Maybe these MacGregor people declined to build a house when there was already one waiting for them inside the earth.

It feels like it's been forever, although my phone's clock

shows we've been down here for about two hours, when we hear sounds up ahead. Voices, several of them. I click my phone shut and don't make a sound. Which would be worse, I wonder; a group of fugitive criminals or a top-secret government operation with orders to silence witnesses?

The voices draw closer. A flicker of light shows that they've got a flashlight, although we aren't directly in its beam. Whoever's holding it is walking quickly, and so are the others. They don't seem like disciplined government agents, or criminals concerned with stealth. They sound more like...high school kids.

Suddenly we're in the beam of the flashlight, and as Kate aims it down we can see Jarri, Willy, and Brandon standing just behind her. I have a million questions, but so do they. We sit down and switch off the flashlight to save battery.

"We've really made a mess of this. None of us should be down here. Did your group manage to find anyone?"

"No", says Kate, "we were hoping you might have. Can't find Ricky, can't find Chase, can't find Trent. No locals, no park rangers, no cops. We've lost the magician *and* his nephew. Plus two hooligans to boot. Not finding a damn thing."

"Just an SUV full of pressurized gas canisters", Jarri adds.

I shake my head, although nobody can see it. "I don't know how to say this. September died shortly before noon."

I hear multiple gasps.

"Danny and I found her lying in the woods. There was nothing we could do. She wasn't dying, she was already dead. I think it looks like homicide. Whoever killed her might be going after the rest of us. How long has it been since anyone actually saw Ricky?"

I can tell they're all thinking about it. I can't remember seeing him since yesterday's hike where Mr. Kretschak almost fell inside the cave. We got back to the campsite, and then what?

"How many light sources do you have?"

"Just the one flashlight. Why?"

"Okay, that's what I was afraid of. Can't split the party. I'm not using this phone to see in the dark anymore if I can help it."

"What happened to the others? Where's Trent?", asks Danny.

"We got caught in a cow stampede. Trent's been badly hurt. Chase is missing too. Plus Ricky from last night. No one's actually seen him since right after we got back from the first cave entrance."

"How'd you get down here? Another entrance?", I ask.

"Yeah", says Jarri. "There was a big rockslide right after the stampede. We found an entrance behind where the rocks fell."

We sit in silence until it gets uncomfortable.

"Okay", says Kate, taking charge, "here's what we know. One of our friends is dead and another three missing, not to mention Mr. Kretschak. Lily and Miranda are still up at the campsite, probably huddled in a tent if it's raining that hard. Miranda still doesn't have her inhaler. Go the way Pedro and Danny came in, and we just arrive at an old still in the middle of the woods. Go back the way we came, and we end up in a ravine way below the road. Think we should try finding another passage? It might come out somewhere closer to civilization."

"That's what frustrates me", I say. "We're only miles from civilization. Not tens or hundreds of miles. If we'd done this better, we'd have made it to somewhere by now where we could get help. If Mr. Kretschak made it back, he's got no way to know where we are."

"Pedro, there's no point blaming anybody for what's happened. We've got to figure out a solution for right now. Figuring out where we went wrong isn't going to do anything."

Surprisingly, it's Danny who says this. My estimation of him goes up.

"You're absolutely right", I reply. "Anybody else got any words of wisdom?"

"Penis", says Willy, like he would in class on a day with a substitute teacher. My estimation of him goes down.

"Can I hit him?", says Kate. "Please?"

"Go ahead."

We all hear the smack. "Ow!", yells Brandon. "That was me!"

"Sorry!"

It sounds like Willy is standing up. "I'm not going to stick around here if you're going to hit me, jerk!"

"Jerk yourself! Sep's dead, this is no time for stupid jokes!"

"Who are you calling stupid, me? You're the idiot that led us into this mess!"

The sounds of footfalls tell me that Willy is storming off in the direction they came from...or maybe a different direction. In the dark. This is not what we need.

"Willy!", I yell, rising. "Get back here!"

"Cows!", comes his defiant reply.

"I'll get him", says Jarri, "just wait here. This thing has enough light."

He pulls something out of his hoodie, hits a button, and produces a faint blue glow. Danny follows as he walks around a bend in the tunnel, and it's amazing how quickly they're out of sight. The glow from Jarri's gadget – some music player, I'll bet – is swallowed up by the gloom and we're back in the dark.

Kate clicks on the flashlight and stands up. Brandon and I rise as well, hoping to catch them quickly. It's not to be. Jarri and Danny are already some forty feet away when a rock comes tumbling out of nowhere and lands with a spectacular crash in the middle of the tunnel. Kate shines the light up to reveal that here the ceiling is quite high – we must be below a large hill – and more rocks are tumbling down from high up.

Everyone screams and ducks for cover. The noise is overpowering. Brandon, Kate, and I tumble and land in a heap in our struggle to get away from the rocks. There's no sign of anyone else. Jarri, Danny, and Willy are either squished underneath those rocks or cut off from us on the other side. On the one hand, Kate has landed so close to me that I can feel her breath on the back of my neck and her tummy moving against my forearm with each breath; on the other hand, my face is jammed into Brandon's armpit and it's not a pleasant place. I'm going to give him a stick of deodorant someday as a gag gift.

"That's the second one today! What's happening?" Kate yells, exasperated, as she pulls herself up. "Seriously, it's like we're in an earthquake zone!"

Now there's something I hadn't thought of. Though I'd be ashamed to admit this to Mr. Kretschak, I don't really know much about earthquake zones in America other than the San Andreas fault. There have been six earthquakes in Colombia during my life, the latest just last month, and Afghanistan gets earthquakes often, but I don't think the eastern United States is seismically active. Still, between the landslide Kate's group encountered – that must have been the distant rumbling Danny and I heard earlier, I realize – and what just happened, something weird is going on.

That's when I recall that in both Colombia and Afghanistan, I've known people who've survived earthquakes because they paid attention to animals who could sense it coming. My tutor Omar claimed that one of the consequences of Adam and Eve being thrown from Eden for listening to the Devil was that humanity lost the ability that all other creatures have to predict earthquakes. Could the cows Kate mentioned have been spooked by a small earthquake about to happen? Could the crash that's separated us from Jarri and Danny have been an aftershock?

"Maybe we *are* in an earthquake zone."

"We're not. Trust me."

"Yeah", pitches in Brandon, "the nearest fault line to here is in Missouri. This area's been geologically dead for a long time."

147

"Okay, but *something*'s seriously wrong. Rocks don't just go crashing around like that for no reason."

"The Heart of the Raven..." Kate muses, her words trailing off. In the pitch black, I wish I could read her expression.

"Come again?"

"Yeah, what did you just say?" Brandon is clearly intrigued.

"I came across that phrase when I was reading up on the history of this area", explains **Kate**, "it has to do with the MacGregors and Roysters."

I tell them what I told Mr. Kretschak the other day in the van, seeming so long ago now. The highwayman families, the supposed caves full of hidden ill-gotten wealth, the rumors of breeding with dogs. The lost cavers in 1849.

"After that, the little hamlet of Cran Ross disappeared from the map. There was a little quarry there, not a coal mine but a stone mine. The Brazen Bar mine, it was called. Nothing like the huge coal mines of the 1890s and 1900s, this was a really small place where only a few dozen people ever worked."

"The Brazen Bar mine?" Pedro's voice is sharp. I can tell he's heard that name before too.

"It's where that creepy gas station guy said the ghosts came from. I couldn't remember at the time if that was the same place, but I'm positive it was."

"Didn't Mr. Kretschak say there were stairs cut into the walls of the pit we found yesterday? Could that have been a mine entrance? It was a small place. You couldn't have fit more than few dozen miners down there. Plus Danny and I found the ruins of a sill near the entrance we came in through. The bottles had "MacGregor" stamped on them."

I suppress a shudder. "Then this has to be the place."

We're in the Heart of the Raven, whatever that means.

Jarri doesn't care where we are, only that we find everyone who's still alive and get out of here. The faint glow from my digital music library, the thing that's usually in the lap pocket of my hoodie, doesn't go that far, but it's just enough to not crash into the walls of the cave. Danny, tagging along a few feet behind me, keeps tripping. I realize he can probably only see the source of my light rather than anything illuminated by it. I try not to block the light.

"Willy!", I yell, hoping he hasn't gone far. I see movement ahead. It's got to be him.

"Jarri?"

The voice answering me, from twenty or thirty feet away, isn't Willy. It's Chase.

"There you are! Kate's so mad at you. Why did you run off like that?"

"Never mind why! Look what I found."

Chase fast-walks toward me and shoves an object into the glow of my light. At the same moment, Danny crashes into me from behind, sending the music player flying out of my hands and landing on the ground, mercifully not breaking the light source. Two seconds later, another figure crashes into Chase from my left side. I grab the light and shine it into Willy's face.

"Okay, can the four of us not get split up again? We're in enough of a mess already. Sep's dead, Trent and Ricky are missing..."

Chase cuts me off, suddenly serious. "Sep's dead? How?"

Danny answers. "I don't know how. Pedro and I couldn't tell what happened to her."

"Down here?"

"No, in the woods. We think someone killed her. They might be after us too."

"It's probably the driver of that SUV we found before the cow stampede", I say, "and I can't shake the feeling that we're right

149

where he wants us to be."

Chase shoves the thing he found back in front of my light. It's a book, leather-bound, old by the looks of it. The pages are yellow and mildewed, but it looks like the ink has held up. What I smell, though, isn't the smell of a mildewy old book.

"Darn it, Chase, are you high?"

"Of course."

"You leave any for me?"

"Didn't know you smoke. Yeah, you give off that vibe, but..."

"Never mind. What is this?", I ask, exasperated.

"It's a journal. Look who it belongs to. I haven't got very far but you've got to see this."

He flips it to the first page and reads it to the rest of us.

"Herein is the journal of Edgar Allan Poe, of Richmond, a seeker after the truth that is to be found in deep darkness."

Even Danny and Willy seem impressed. "Whoa...", one of them whispers behind me.

"So far it's all been a record of his dreams. I haven't read too many of his stories but I remember reading the Murders in the Rue Morgue early freshman year. It's a murder mystery. Four or five people overheard it and they each tell the cops that the killer was speaking a different language. They finally figure out that everybody was guessing a language that they didn't recognize, because it was actually an orangutan. Well, look at this."

Chase points to an entry on the third page. Written in a scrawling hand is a paragraph describing the dream experience of hearing a mysterious voice through a door and trying to figure out what the person is saying, then opening the door and finding a strange reddish beast snarling and tearing a person apart.

"Wait", I say, "so Poe turned his dreams into short stories?"

Chase nods. "That's what it looks like."

"How would his journal get down here?", asks Danny.

"This is how. It was always down here. He came to this cave dozens of times. Called it the Dark Heart of the Raven. Look. Poe explains here what he did for inspiration. He'd come down here with lantern, turn it off, and just sit here in the dark for a while. He'd dream while he was still awake. Says here he'd see things that weren't there but were still true. Don't quite get what that means. Sounds kinda cool though. Then he'd turn the lantern back on and write down what he'd seen."

In my ancestral culture, it dawns on me, Poe would be called a shaman. I'm reminded of Kate's strange words about sitting still in the dark and facing our fears.

Danny, in the dim light, looks really serious. "We've been reading Poe stories in Mr. Ward's class. He told us that Poe wrote a book where some people are on a lifeboat out in the ocean. They're starving. They're out of food and water. To survive, they have to kill a guy and eat him. They become something monstrous, Mr. Ward said, they cease to be human in order to live. I thought that was really deep. Anyway, the guy's name is Richard Parker. Thirty years or something after Poe wrote that story, the ship that they wrote *Moby Dick* about sank, and four guys ended up in a rowboat with no food or water just like in Poe's story. So they killed a guy and ate him, in real life. That guy's name was also Richard Parker."

"Wait," says Chase, "isn't that the name of the tiger in..."

"Yeah, it is. Anyway, some people think Poe could predict the future. I wonder what else we might find in here."

"Well," Chase admits, "I saw a little bit of the last page. Poe says he got lost down here and met creatures down here. They were like wolves, walking on two legs..."

Everyone shudders. This would be cool if we weren't actually stuck in the same cave. We've got to find a way out of here.

"Yeah," Chase continues, "I didn't want to read that part."

"Okay," says **Kate**, "let's put this together. What if the legends are true somehow? A pack of wild dogs running around down here. People living down here, gone completely animalistic, or intentionally trying to live like werewolves. It could happen. There are people in Europe today who choose to be vampires. They live in caves in Transylvania and as far as anyone knows they actually drink human blood. Once in a while a journalist goes missing while looking for them. I've also read that there were religions in that part of the world in ancient times where people would live as werewolves for a while. So it could be something like that going on here. Only thing is, nobody knows if those ancient mystery religions involved choice or coercion."

"So..." Pedro says, hesitantly, "they could be giving someone a drug, or infecting them with a disease, that makes them run around like wild animals for a while?"

"Like Nebuchadnezzar in the Bible", says Brandon.

"I'd never thought of that", Pedro adds.

"Yeah, that kind of thing, I guess. Seems like it wears off eventually. Someone could get caught for a few months or a few years and then escape once the effects wear off...oh my gosh.

"That guy you found in the woods wasn't the driver of the vehicle! He was someone who they had infected or drugged or just lured in somehow, but he escaped, and they were trying to bring him back."

"What do you mean, lured in?" Pedro asks.

"The same way people kidnap kids. Free candy, help me find my lost puppy, get in my van."

Brandon is skeptical. "I don't think that happens in real life."

"But tourists get lured into situations like that all the time. Cute girls stand out on the sidewalk to lure guys into bars where their boyfriends force the victim to drink way too much and then they mug him. My cousin fell for that scam once in Amsterdam. Got a black eye when he tried to leave."

Pedro sighs. "Maybe they use weed as bait. They'd definitely have Chase by now."

"Well, I'm serious. Sep, Ricky, Trent, and Chase were all involved in stealing beer from another campsite the first night. Now Sep's dead and those three boys are missing. Any of them could have been offered alcohol or drugs and taken captive. They don't have good enough judgment to resist."

Brandon protests. "Trent can't even stand up right now."

"So? He's not thinking straight. You had your back turned, Jarri and I were out of the room, and that leaves Willy the witless wonder in charge of watching Trent. Somebody comes up to him, offers him something to dull the pain – why wouldn't he take it?"

"I think I'm leaning in a different direction", says Pedro. "Remember the meeting we had last month, right before they decided to let Chase go on the trip? What if Lily was right? What if there are other species of humans, adapted to living in caves? What if some of them live here?"

"Sounds like a horror flick", says Brandon dismissively.

"And this doesn't already feel like one? This isn't the only place I've heard of this. There are legends in the Andes of human-like creatures living in caves deep in the mountains. My grandfather told me when I was eight that he found one once. In Afghanistan, my tutor told me there are dog-headed people living underground in different parts of the world."

I've heard plenty of such stories, and tend to believe them too. "What if we're both right? What if these 'invisible ghosts' are a different species of human, driven underground thousands of years ago, and kidnapping and drugging people is important to their survival somehow?"

"Then God help us."

"Preferably right now", adds Brandon, clicking on the light.

I look. There's a real dog-headed man standing five feet away.

16: TOWER

These kids are a disgrace. I can see them, all of them plus the adult in charge – and I'm *not* counting Miranda as an adult – from right here. They've already found one entrance this afternoon, and it's only a matter of time before they find more. My brother has no idea what he's unleashed. Until today, neither did I.

It is a strange thing, to be at the controls of so much power and yet feel so powerless. Here in my technological tower, I am the master of all the information I could desire. The problem isn't that I can see the disaster approaching hours before it starts happening, or that I can take not a single action to prevent any of it.

No, the problem is that I am not the only one who sees everything that's going on.

*****

David leads Thomas into the classroom. Mrs. Abischer, the ancient history teacher, is inside, gathering materials on her way out. It is, after all, her prep room. Thomas notices, uncomfortably, that David's body language is pressuring Mrs. Abischer to leave. She isn't taking the hint. Mrs. Abischer is one of those teachers who thinks the teachers' lounge should be a place to chat and talk and ask other teachers questions about everything. Others on the faculty would rather have it be a place where they *don't* get asked tons of questions and forced to talk and talk and talk, since they get enough of that in class already.

"I heard somebody yelling out there", says Mrs. Abischer in the same not-particularly-serious tone of voice that students use to discuss the latest juicy gossip. "Who was it?"

Thomas sighs. "Creighton. Chase Creighton. That kid is just...I don't even know how to put it. He's got a few screws loose."

Mrs. Abischer chuckled. "Yeah, he's in my second-hour class on Tuesdays and Thursdays. A couple weeks ago, the kids were getting kind of squirrely, and I asked, 'Does anybody want to get a detention?' – and guess what Chase does? He sticks up his hand."

Thomas sort of laughs. "Did you give him one?"

Mrs. Abischer shrugs. "Well, I didn't want to make an empty threat..."

David's not in the mood for gossip. Besides, he already knows about this. The detention log is something he reads every weekend, for fun, except that David doesn't have fun.

Which is the main reason Ricky doesn't get along with him.

Mrs. Abischer sort of takes the hint and leaves, but not before wishing them a nice day and all those other pleasantries that David despises. He isn't smiling as he closes the door firmly.

Thomas gulps. This isn't going to be good.

David rounds on him. "Do you realize that you've already given me justification to cancel this trip?"

Thomas looks more confused than angry, which isn't what David was expecting. "Cancel the trip? Why?"

"You got in an argument with Cunningham and humiliated him in front of other students over creationism? What the hell were you thinking? Do you know where we are? Hello? Kentucky suburbs of Cincinnati, does that ring any bells?"

Thomas starts to interrupt. This kind of sarcasm is not constructive. There's even a line in the faculty handbook about that.

"Do you realize who our major donors are? Do you realize the kind of funding we could lose if these people find out that one of our teachers humiliates kids for believing the same things they do?"

"I did not humiliate him!"

"He says you did. This isn't the first complaint I've had about you. I've had several parents come to me this year already about you. They say that you..."

Thomas interrupts him for real this time. "Who? When? This is the first time I've ever heard about anyone having a problem with

155

me. Why would they go to you anyway? You're not my department chair...you're not even really *in* my department, now that we separated math and science last year!"

"It's none of your business who they are. The point is that I've had complaints about you, and I need to do something."

"No, David. Complaints about me are none of *your* business. If someone has a problem with me, I would expect them to contact me immediately. I have not had a *single* complaint email this year. Or last year. I can show you dozens of emails I get from parents thanking me for..."

"Thomas, you are on thin enough ice already."

Thomas ignores his brother. "...all of the good work that I do in their kids' lives. If someone is having a less positive experience of me, they should contact me right away so I can fix the problem. It's in the handbook. Look it up."

David shrugs. "I don't care."

Before Thomas can respond, David continues. "Cunningham is thinking about contacting the local news to report that a teacher harassed him for his beliefs. At a Christian school, for crying out loud! Berghall does not need that kind of publicity."

"Calling the news? What a little shit."

"And *that's* the other thing I need to talk to you about! You watch your fucking language! I cannot be*lieve* what I just heard you say to Creighton out in the hallway."

"I didn't say anything to him. *He* yelled at *me*."

"No, you called him a derogatory epithet. You're just doing *wonders* for this school's image today."

"Derogatory epithet? I didn't..."

"I heard exactly what you said."

"I don't even remember what I said."

"I bet you use that defense all the time."

"No, I don't get attacked all the time."

"You're going to tell me what was going on there."

"Fine. I subbed for Mrs. Hutton's class earlier today and, well, it was Chase along with Trent Jackson. They each had a whiteboard marker..."

"How did they get them?"

"Well, gosh, I guess they extended their arms, opened their fingers, grabbed the markers, and picked them up. They had them by the time I was done checking attendance. Didn't do anything bad with them until halfway through class."

"Oh, that makes it so much better."

"David, do you want me to tell you what happened, or are you just going to keep interrupting me?"

David glares at Thomas, prompting him to continue.

*****

If it were just the thirteen of them, it would all be under my control. But now someone else is watching them too, and they've got better technology. And easy access to get boots on the ground nearby. This is spiraling out of control. For the first time, I start to wonder if I handled this properly.

*****

"Okay, like I was saying, Chase and Trent..."

"Creighton and Jackson."

"...each had a marker. I was writing something on the board with another marker, I turned around to face the class, and they were each holding their marker in their laps, under a rag, shaking it like..."

Thomas picks up a marker and, holding it straight in front of himself, shakes it lengthwise back and forth, vigorously.

"...but in their laps, you know?"

David glares at him. "So they were pretending to masturbate in your class."

"Mrs. Hutton's class, but yes, you would have to put it so bluntly, wouldn't you?"

"I'm more concerned about what happened just now in the hallway. You were talking to Alvarez, almost as if here were another teacher..."

"Well, he is eighteen, and potential valedictorian, should I really be treating him like a kid?"

"...and you described this encounter to him that should have been kept under wraps. You did so using a derogatory word. Creighton heard you. That's two kids you've insulted today."

"What word are you talking about?!"

"The f-word."

"I don't say that word in front of students."

"The *other* f-word."

Thomas has to think about it for a second. "I might have referred to them as maggots. I did *not* say..."

"I distinctly heard you! Creighton heard it too!"

Well, thinks Thomas glumly, at least that makes a little more sense why Chase got so mad.

"Sensitivity training 101, Thomas. You *do not* use words like that in a school setting."

"You have nothing to talk to me about sensitivity. Or tolerance. What would your son have to say about..."

"You leave Richard out of this!"

"Not him. Your *other* son."

David slaps Thomas so hard that he expects other teachers to walk in wondering if a bookshelf fell over.

"I have *one* son! And he's not involved in this!"

Thomas, his face red and stinging, is severely tempted to hit back. To knock David to the floor, to have the brother-versus-brother all-out fight that they never had growing up because of their age difference. He has never been so angry at anyone in his life.

*****

Oh, so now Miranda left her inhaler behind. Such a child. She has no business leading actual children. This is playing into my hands better than I had even expected.

*****

"Fuck you, David! You have *nothing* to say about sensitivity! Not to me, not to anyone! You're such a hypocrite! I have bent over backwards – okay, bad choice of words – gone to great lengths to be an ally to the gay kids at this school. We *do* have those! Do you have *any fucking idea* how hard people like you make their lives? Those kids show up to school every day and get told that they're inferior, they're sinners, they're second-class citizens at best. That they have to deny themselves a major element of life just because some people won't tolerate them."

David looks like he's just had an epiphany. "Like you, in other words."

Thomas says nothing.

"You are, aren't you? That explains a lot."

"That's none of your business."

David can tell he's hit the mark, and Thomas can tell that David has finally noticed. Thirty-three years old, not married, never even had a girlfriend...how did David, or their parents, not put this together earlier?

"Oh, I get it now. You're trying to stop homosexual kids from having the same lonely, unfulfilling life that you have."

"My life is perfectly fulfilling. I love my job."

"That's a pity. You might not have it much longer."

"You have no power over that."

"For now. You know the headmaster is retiring at the end of the year. Why shouldn't I be a likely candidate to succeed him?"

"Because you're a piece of shit?"

"Don't make me hit you again."

"I'll tell Mom and Dad."

For a moment, it *almost* seems like David might laugh. But he doesn't. He looks at the ceiling, almost thoughtfully.

"The trip, meanwhile. What a disaster waiting to happen. You in charge, me not around to restore order. One adult barely worthy to be called that, out in the wilds of West Virginia with a bunch of kids. What could possibly go wrong?"

"Um, not *one* adult. Four, technically, since Kate and Pedro are eighteen. Obviously I'm not the only teacher going. Miss Stillman? Remember her? About five-foot six, dark blonde..."

"Oh yes, I certainly do remember Miss Miranda Stillman. You know what happened the last time she was on this trip."

Thomas groans. "That's completely irrelevant."

David shakes his head. "*Nothing* is irrelevant."

*****

Oh, Thomas, what are you planning to do? How many safety protocols have you broken already today, and how many more are you breaking now?

The view on one of my screens now shows the woods

whizzing by. Thomas must be driving the van, alone, and he's going awfully fast. I wonder how much longer he'll stay in control.

*****

"So you're going to hold Miranda's past against her?"

"No, I'm holding her present against her. She does not belong on the faculty at this school."

"I don't know what you mean. The kids all like her..."

"Students do not need to like their teachers. They need to *respect* them. Nothing else matters. With a teacher that young, popularity with the students is not a mark in the teacher's favor. It means that person is failing to conduct herself as a proper authority figure."

"It does not."

"What you think does not matter. Miranda will not get her entry contract renewed next year."

"You're awfully optimistic."

"That's not a prediction. It's already been decided. She will be departing this institution at the end of the school year."

"She hasn't mentioned this to me."

"She doesn't know. She will be informed at the beginning of May. One month's notice is more than generous."

"Bullshit."

"And another thing. If she finds out earlier than that, I will know that it was you who informed her. If she resigns over Christmas break, or if I get a *hint* that she's looking for a new job prior to being formally notified of my decision, you also will get to look for a new job. And don't count on a recommendation."

Thomas is almost beside himself. He feels like he's been struck by lightning. This can't be happening. How can so much of what he's worked for be disintegrating, just like this? And over what? He hasn't even done anything wrong.

"I don't know whether you'll be here either next year, Thomas. You have the remainder of this year to prove yourself worthy of teaching at Berghall. Once I'm in charge, there are going to be some changes here."

"You mean, changes to the tenure system that we've had in place since the school was founded?"

"Exactly. My, you *are* catching on. No teacher will ever get more than a year contract at a time starting next year."

"I can't believe what I'm hearing."

"I can't believe I'm about to let you go to West Virginia without a legitimate authority figure present. You, and that irresponsible twenty-three-year-old girl? If I let you take those kids along, it's going to be a total disaster."

*****

It's turned out worse than I could have expected. Kids drinking underage and causing a ruckus was supposed to happen. Kids panicking and scattering into the woods was not. I need to do something. But what?

*****

"I have faith in them. The older ones, at least."

"Your 'faith' is misplaced. Not to worry, I will cure you of it."

Thomas sighs and balls up his fists. "So you're canceling my trip?"

"No. You will lead it in October, this one last time, the outcome of which will be the justification for not offering it in the future. And just to make sure you behave yourself, you'll be taking that little *maggot* Creighton along with you."

17: STAR

We can't help it. **Pedro**, Kate, and Brandon scream and run away from the thing we've just seen. Five and a half feet tall, but its body coiled and tensed as if ready to pounce, bipedal, its arms clearly ending in claws, its head that of a dog or wolf or similar creature, there's no way this thing wasn't real. It wasn't standing still either. Not a statue or a weirdly mounded carcass. This was most assuredly a creature of flesh and blood, alive and breathing.

"Okay, you guys saw what I saw, right?"

Panting, scared out of our wits, we come to a halt several twists and turns later. Kate has the flashlight and was in the middle of us as we ran, so we managed not to crash into the walls or ceiling of the passage. Still, we're as dazed as if we'd all been hit over the head with something heavy.

"Yeah", says Kate. "It was alive."

"It was trying to communicate with us", says Brandon.

"Communicate what? 'Mmm, you look delicious'?"

"Pedro, if it wanted to eat us, it would have. Surely it can find its way in the dark better than we can. There's no way we outran it."

Kate whips the flashlight around, finding nothing. The creature, whatever it was, hasn't followed us. Or if it has, it's at a distance. Not a comforting thought.

"Shit", I mumble, "I have no idea where we are. Are we back where we lost Jarri and Danny?"

"I don't think so", says Kate.

"I was hoping you'd say yes."

"Shh. I hear something."

Brandon and I fall silent. There it is, unmistakable. A moaning sound, from the direction opposite the way we came

163

running from the wolfman. Maybe it knew a quicker way and got around us. Maybe these things hunt in packs. Or maybe...

"It's Trent!", Brandon whispers.

The sound is definitely that of someone waking up in a bit of pain, tired and confused. Light forward, **Kate** strides carefully to the source of the moans.

There's someone lying there in an awkward heap, just barely awake and trying to figure out their surroundings, but it's not Trent.

It's Lily.

"Are you okay?", I ask, putting a reassuring hand on her shoulder. She blinks, yawns, and flinches, but looks me in the eye with recognition.

"I don't know", she drawls slowly, looking woozy. "I feel like I got hit over the head. Probably did."

"What do you remember? Where's Miranda?"

I hate to demand anything from her while she's visibly half-asleep and confused, but we have to get her to talk. Pedro and Brandon sit down on either side of me, concern in their faces.

"I was walking a little ways into the trees. Miss Stillman was sitting by the campfire ring. She was doing okay, like she wasn't having any more asthma trouble. I snuck off to...well, you know...I wasn't going to be gone long. Never heard anything. I had just found a spot and was about to...why do there have to be boys listening to this?...I still had my pants on and was just about to go quickly when all of a sudden I'm lying facedown on the ground and my head hurts unbelievably. Still does. Next thing I knew, I'm here."

I shine the flashlight on the sides and back of her head. There's a little swelling, but it doesn't look too serious.

"Does this hurt?" I poke her.

"No."

"What about this?"

"No, that's fine."

"What about this?"

"Ow!"

"Good. If that didn't hurt, it'd mean you have a concussion."

"So you think I don't?

"Doesn't look like it. Still, somebody or something hit you over the head. They could have been hitting harder, though."

"Then they dragged me down here? Why?"

"I don't know why. But at least you're with us."

"What about Miss Stillman?", asks Brandon, concerned.

"I don't know where she is. If they got her, they didn't leave her near me."

Whatever else we might have said is interrupted by an insistent growl from the way Pedro and Brandon and I came from. I shine the flashlight at its source. A knife finds its way from my pocket into my other hand.

The creature standing there looks more like a man than a wolf, different from the thing that we ran from a few minutes ago. Still, he's absolutely savage-looking. His skin is incredibly pale, eyes white, teeth sharp, and clothing utterly ragged. The nails on his hands are claw-like and sharp, and it looks like the hands have dewclaws outside of the pinkies. But at least I would call them hands, rather than paws. The strange being stares at us for what seems eternity.

Then he does the last thing any of us were expecting. He speaks. In English.

"Fear not. Harm I intend you not."

"He's an angel!", Lily whispers.

I shush her, although his words do sound familiar.

"Come with me you must. Follow."

"Why?", Pedro asks, positioning himself between the pale man and the rest of us, looking ready for a fight.

The cave creature, if that's really what he is, looks thoughtful and cocks his head to the side. "Know this word I not."

They have no concept of "why"? I try to imagine how that's even possible.

"Come with me you must. Show you, I intend. Show you Star Chamber."

That doesn't sound good. A place where people make really arbitrary decisions and don't explain to anyone why? Actually, that sounds just like our school.

"You won't hurt us?", Pedro asks suspiciously.

"Harm I intend you not!", the creature insists.

Without waiting for a reply, our new acquaintance turns around and walks away. I try not to gasp when we see that he has a tail, about a foot long and covered in fur like his legs and feet. Lily either doesn't try not to gasp, or fails.

"We've got to follow him", I say, striding forward with the flashlight. I don't want to lose sight of the creature, whatever it is he's trying to show us. It can't be worse than what would happen to us if we never found our way out at all.

"Follow me you choose. Please me. Learn our ways. Hear our tale. Be safe inside Star Chamber."

Intrigued, I keep up his pace. The creature seems to be either blind or able to see in the dark. As my flashlight beam moves across him and brightens up the tunnel ahead of him, there's no reaction. He doesn't seem to mind the light, which is encouraging. I look behind me and confirm that Brandon, Danny, and Lily are following.

"Tale very long", the creature says, turning to face me as he walks. "Long walk. I tell you tale."

"Okay", I say, trying to find some way to express agreement that he will understand. Clearly he doesn't have as wide a range of grammar and vocabulary as the rest of us do. Whether that's because he's had few ways to learn English – probably from captives, I surmise – or because his species simply doesn't use as complex of language as other people, I can't begin to guess.

"Long age back. Mother beyond mother beyond mothers back. Our people live on sky lands. You come. You hunt great beasts. You hunt our people. Our people intend peace. Harm our people intend you not. You listen not. You harm our people."

He's not explaining it in fresh terms, I realize, but reciting an old story. Maybe a *very* old story, usually told in a different language. It occurs to me that he might not understand "you" as a pronoun; it might simply be their word for humans. For modern humans, I mean. Whatever he is, even with the tail and dewclaws, he's clearly human. Genus Homo, species something other than sapiens.

Pedro draws even with me, Lily and Brandon still hanging back. "He's telling us a story from the stone age", Pedro whispers to me, "can you believe how awesome this is?"

Led by the creature, we round a bend, and there before us is the more canine-looking creature we saw earlier. It growls, baring fangs. The head is decidedly wolf-like, with an elongated snout and the ears much higher up on the head than on our guide. Yet, the canine creature is also bipedal. It has the same hands and feet, with claw-like nails and dewclaws but clearly human-shaped even so.

The more human creature growls and snarls a little at the canine, which responds by lowering its head in a gesture of submission.

"Fear not. Skash intend harm not. Skash obey me."

Skash, the wolf-like creature, slinks away, and we walk forward, still following the human creature. To our discomfort, Skash takes up the rear, walking only a few feet behind Brandon. If he's guarding or escorting us, it's not the most reassuring way to be escorted.

Our guide continues. "Our people leave sky lands. Our people live in dark lands. Our people walk in ice lands. Our people come on new lands. New lands akin to sky lands. Our people see. Our people breathe wind and touch trees. You come. You hunt great beasts. You hunt our people. Our people sad. No new home akin to sky lands. Our people live in dark lands again."

The way he's saying it, so formula-driven, emotionless, confirms my suspicions that he's telling an old story that's been drilled into generations upon generations of creatures like him. They once lived aboveground in Asia or Europe, before modern humans arrived and treated them like animals. Some of them hid in caves in the places they originally lived, while others made their way across the Arctic to the Americas. They were safe there until our species found its way here, twelve thousand years ago. Now they have lived in caves so long that they've become pale and blind like other creatures adapted to cave life. But somehow they've kept the old memories alive. It's incredible.

We're going deep into the heart of the mountain, the floor visibly sloping down and down. I look behind me at my companions, and confirm that Skash is still trailing the group, keeping a watchful eye over us. I'm as nervous as anybody else here, but for Lily's sake and Brandon's I try not to show it.

"Our people change. Our people see not. You come not. Our people live safe. High Priestess tell our tale every gathering."

"That makes sense", I whisper to Pedro, who I'm sure has been following his story as closely as I have. "They have an elder whose job is to maintain the story and make sure it gets told properly every year so the people remember it."

"Every year? How would they keep track of years down here? There are no seasons inside a cave."

Pedro's right. Do the creatures hold their gatherings on some other kind of timetable? I don't know if animals that spend their whole lives in the dark have circadian rhythms, and suddenly I'm wondering if anyone's ever studied that. Would sentient, basically human beings living in caves still have daily or yearly cycles? Any cycles at all? There have to be some kind of rhythms down here, don't there?

"Our people get sick. Our people have babies not. Our people choose. Die or break old taboo? Our people choose break taboo. Our people mate wolves. Our people have babies with wolves. Babies with wolves have babies not. Babies with wolves hunt. Babies with wolves bring food. Our people die not."

Pedro and I share astonished looks. Our guide has just admitted that some part of the stories I'd heard about interbreeding with wolves or dogs is true. Human-wolf hybrids obviously can't reproduce, but here it looks like they can survive as viable creatures and live long enough to do the hunting for their human relatives. I realize that Skash must be one such creature. Human enough to walk on two feet and decently intelligent, but canine enough to have a strong pack instinct and be totally obedient to the non-hybrid leaders.

But surely the human creatures must also breed offspring who can reproduce, or they'd still die out after a generation, whenever this crisis that he's describing happened. Unless they're immortal, the thought suddenly occurs to me.

The guide has been walking so long – it must be evening if not actually night by now – that when he stops in his tracks, it gets our attention. I look around and realize we must be a very long ways down below ground. The whole geology of the cavern around us is different. Above us, the roof twinkles with a thousand points of light as my flashlight beam sweeps across it, looking like stars.

"Diamonds", Pedro whispers to me.

"A girl's best friend", I reply almost instinctively, before my brain can catch up with my mouth and think about what message I'm sending him. The look on his face is priceless.

"Star Chamber", the guide announces. "I Mabov. I bring you

inside Star Chamber. Very few you ever inside Star Chamber."

My theory that he's using "you" to translate a word for modern humans has just been confirmed.

"Stay here you must", says Mabov. "Safe inside Star Chamber. Sky lands ruined. Fire burn sky lands. Water flood sky lands. Air foul sky lands."

"How long do we stay here?", asks Pedro. I'm hoping as much as he is that the answer isn't "forever".

Mabov shrugs. "You leave when ready. You meet the white raven. You meet the High Priestess."

"The white raven?", asks Brandon. "That's me. My name means 'raven' and I'm white even though my family is black. So who's the High Priestess?"

I don't answer, because I think off in the distance, in the middle of the massive room we're in, I'm seeing the High Priestess.

*****

Jarri is so tired of running. We were getting somewhere on reading Edgar Allan Poe's journal, when suddenly there was a noise about fifteen or twenty meters away that didn't come from the four of us. Willy panicked and ran. Then Danny panicked and ran in the other direction. Now Chase and I are trying to stick together, in dim light, wondering if we have any chance of catching either of those idiots. They're running around in total darkness. We're just in *almost* total darkness.

At least the ground here is level, I think, just in time to see Chase trip. He lands, screams, silences the scream, and backs up, crashing into me. I try not to touch him any more than I have to, just putting a hand on his shoulder to let him know where I am, remembering what happened earlier today when Kate tried to give him a hand up.

"What?", I ask. Then I look down, and stop wondering.

It's Trent. He's lying on the floor of the cave, unmistakably dead. The deep cuts in his chest and abdomen were too much to heal. His face, at least, looks peaceful enough. It seems like he wasn't in much pain at the end. But he's dead all the same. And so is Ricky, lying a few feet away, something stuck in the middle of his forehead that seems to have killed him.

This is too much. Three people dead. I feel like I've known for the last few hours that Trent wasn't going to make it and Ricky was probably murdered last night, but finding confirmation is just the most awful feeling.

Three lives, so full of promise, gone. Snuffed out, just like that. And for what? Why would someone kill September and Ricky and Trent?

"They must have known something", I muse. "Whoever killed them was trying to silence them. They had seen something, some secret that had to be kept hidden. But what?"

Chase is totally numb at this point. Trent wasn't my childhood friend, but he's become the only person I can depend on for these last few months. I can't believe it ended like this. I was supposed to be living at his house all year, and maybe senior year too; there's no way I can ever go back to my old high school in Paducah. Not after all the stupid shit I did last year. Not that I'd want to, after freshman year.

Jarri's right, though. Somebody doesn't just murder three teenagers without a reason. Is there something down here, or in the woods aboveground, that's so valuable or dangerous that it's worth killing over?

"Whatever it is," I realize, "we probably saw it too. We have to get out of these caves."

"I'm not sure about that. Down here might be the only place we're safe."

"But the bodies are down here."

"Look up. Do you see a ceiling?"

I don't. Jarri's electronic beam doesn't go nearly high enough, but it looks like we're at the bottom of a deep underground shaft. There might be hundreds of feet of open air above us before the ground.

"And see this. They look like they were dropped from high up. Whoever killed them didn't come down where we are. They threw them over an underground cliff. This is just where they dispose of the bodies."

"So why was Sep in the woods, where Pedro and Danny found her? Wouldn't they have thrown her down here too?"

"Maybe they were going to. Maybe they've thrown her down a different shaft by now."

"Trent had a will written, you know. He showed it to me."

"Why?", Jarri asks.

"I don't know why. The only thing on it was stipulating what to do with his body…he didn't say anything about his possessions."

"Cremation?"

"Taxidermy."

"I could probably do it here", says Jarri. "Lots of experience with squirrels and rabbits."

I shudder. "Can we at least get away from here? Find another place to sit? Maybe we just need to wait for someone to find us."

Jarri shrugs. "Seems as good a plan as any."

I can't believe what's happening. How did we manage to get so lost and go so wrong, so fast?

We move onward, either toward rescue or getting ourselves even more hopelessly lost. I almost don't care what happens. My life is such a mess. Memories of two years ago flash painfully across my mind…and body. It's unbearable. The pain, the shame, the horrible feeling of wanting to shed my body like a snakeskin and start anew.

The sound of distant running water gets my attention after half an hour or so of walking. Jarri hears it too.

"Okay, that might be our way out. Want to rest up a little before we try go for it?"

I think that sounds good. I'm worn out. Still have a granola bar in my pocket, the kind that's actually two granola bars in one sleeve. The good kind, too, made of real granola without weird preservatives and crap. I offer one to Jarri. He accepts.

"Hmm," says Jarri, halfway through his bar. "That running water sound is really getting to me. Suddenly have to pee real bad."

A shudder and an outbreak of goosebumps would not be a normal guy's reaction to that, but I'm not a normal guy. It shouldn't be a big deal. I pee on parked cars regularly. Why would it frighten me if another guy pees in front of me?

"Just aim that way. I don't want to see it."

"Oh please. I'm not going to splash you with pee."

"No, I mean your penis. I'm terrified of them."

Jarri sighs. "You really haven't figured this out?"

"Figured what out?"

"Chase, I don't *have* a penis."

"What do you mean? What happened to it?"

"I never had one. You ever see my legal name on an attendance sheet? It's not Jarri. It's Jana."

"That sounds like a girl's name."

"Yeah, it is. I have a vagina. The doctor saw that when I was born and decided that I was a girl. My parents always believed her."

I'm speechless. Jarri, the guy who belts out death metal lyrics in a low growl; Jarri, the guy who I've heard flipped over a table in the cafeteria last spring and supposedly defended his actions with "What Would Jesus Do?"; Jarri, the textbook illustration of a brutish caveman, is biologically female? How in the heck...

That's when it occurs to me that Jarri always wears a hoodie and baggy pants. Loose, formless clothes that hide his shape. Especially his chest. Wow.

"Kate said something to me earlier today about facing our fears," Jarri says haggardly, "alone in the dark, by the banks of an underground river, the place where we can't hide from the truth."

"I don't follow."

"I'll explain after I go over there and take a leak."

He goes far enough away that I don't hear anything. I sit there in the darkness, listening to nothing but the drip-drip-drip of water upon rock. I feel like I'm in some gigantic, primal womb. I'm something less than alive yet, formless and void, waiting for the earth to birth me into life above ground. Out there, I will gain form and being. Down here, I have no sight until Jarri returns with the faint glow he carries, no sound until he returns and speaks to me. Alone, I'm surrounded by darkness and almost total silence. Nothing down here but my feelings and thoughts. And memories.

It's been two years. The pain, I now know, will never go away. I can never exorcise the terror and horror of what they did to me. But I haven't even tried. I've been running for two years, two years of endless fight-or-flight, lashing out at everyone around me. Lashing out at my parents, who don't believe me. Lashing out at my friends, who shame me. My teachers, who must know, but don't offer any support; my sister, too good and innocent to understand; my pastor, too vain and corrupt to care. I've declared war on every one of them.

And for what? Do I want to only spread my pain until it infects everyone around like a viral Eucharist with me as the host?

No, I realize, for the first time since freshman year. Really, this is the first time I've thought about what I'm doing instead of just doing whatever pops into my head. I don't want to spread my pain. I want to prevent it from touching anyone else. I've kept it inside by doing one stupid thing after another, keeping my mind from dealing with it, distracting myself day after week after month.

I've been so afraid, for two years, that the person I once was is dead. There is no Chase Gavin Creighton. He's dead, murdered by the upperclassmen bullies who took the humiliation of younger students too far. Whatever I am now, whoever this person is that occupies the same body as Chase, I'm not Chase. I'm what's left of him. If there's anything left of him at all.

Now I understand exactly what Kate and Jarri were talking about. Each of us carries a different burden, but each may set it down only in places like this…cave? The word seems inadequate. Pressure cooker. Alchemy lab. Test tube. Womb. Tomb. Cathedral. My brain shoots off one word after another.

Jarri's back. "Don't tell anyone what you've learned, okay, Chase? I would never feel safe over here if anyone knew."

"Knew what?"

I hope my tone conveys what it's supposed to, that I know what he means but don't even consider it an issue. It seems to work.

"Thank you, Chase. You're the first person I've ever told who didn't think it was a big deal."

"What do your parents think?"

He sighs. "They don't think at all anymore. They're dead."

"I'd say I'm sorry to hear that, but you're probably sick of people saying that."

"Yeah. You've got me figured out."

"No I don't", I say. "I don't even have myself figured out."

"It's rough enough back in Finland, you know. We have better protection there than over here, but it's still not great. I'd have to be sterilized before the law will recognize me as male, and the law won't allow that until I'm eighteen. So I'm trapped, just like every other trans kid in the country. I'll have to deal with that when I go home, assuming I ever do. As long as I'm here, I wonder every day if today's the day…I'm sorry about the other evening, if it didn't seem like I cared about what you were saying about high school sports stars and…"

I cut him off. "Don't say the r-word."

"Okay. But you know I'm afraid of that. If the wrong person found out about my body…"

"You can't be afraid of anything I haven't already been through. And I'm physically male. It can happen to anyone, Jarri. *Anyone.*"

He doesn't speak for a long while.

"Like you said a little while ago," Jarri finally breaks the silence, "you're probably sick and tired of people saying how sorry they are."

"Forget that. I don't want anyone else to know. Best move on and pretend it didn't happen."

"Don't worry about me telling anyone. Besides, we have a saying in my country: those things you learn without joy, you will forget easily. Give me a week or two and I won't even remember."

*****

Pedro can see only darkness nearby, dim light high above. The sky above me sparkles with faint stars, except it isn't a sky and they aren't stars. I'm in the room with the diamonds, but I can't see any sign of Kate. Or Brandon or Lily, for that matter, or even our troglodyte guides Mabov and Skash. I turned my back on them for a few moments, and when I turned back, everyone was gone.

But I'm not alone down here, I can feel that. There's ample energy around me, of several life forces with considerable awareness and curiosity. I whirl around and around, trying to get a visual on the creatures around me. All I can see is the water in small pools in the floor, each slightly glowing in a different color, spaced evenly from each other like a giant multicolored chessboard. There's a low humming, murmuring noise in almost every direction, and it's coming closer.

"Fire comes."

I jump around and find myself face to face with Mabov.

"Fire comes. Our people safe inside Star Chamber. You safe inside Star Chamber."

I won't bother trying to figure out how he speaks English. What he means by "fire" is more important.

"What's going to happen?"

Mabov squints and tilts his head. "Earth poisoned. Fire burn sky lands. Water flood sky lands. Air foul sky lands. The mother protects her children. Evil ones the mother intends harm."

"So you're trying to save us from…"

I realize he's never going to put it in terms that a twenty-first-century person would use. Is he talking about global warming? Pollution? Both? I have an uneasy feeling that he doesn't mean something general; he means something specific that we'd be in danger from above ground, or higher up within the caves. At least that means we're not going to be kept here forever.

Okay, I tell myself, think. Kate's group ran into a stampeding herd of cows. They were scared by something. Danny and I heard no birds and saw no wildlife. All the animals around here are afraid of something, but what? Kate and Brandon told me this part of the country doesn't get earthquakes.

But what about…

Fire burning the earth above ground. The air fouled by its smoke. The mother, Mother Earth, protecting her children, the cave dwellers, and harming the evil ones above the surface…

Now I know why they brought us down here. They really are

trying to save us. The diamonds lining this chamber are the surest protection against what's coming. If only I could get all the others down here…but this place is huge. For all I know, creatures have found Jarri and Danny and Willy and Chase and the rest, and brought them down here too.

"I don't see my friends. Where are they?"

Mabov gestures around him, pointing at something in the dark. "All you we intend no harm, inside Star Chamber."

I hope that means what I think it does.

Because right at this moment, I can hear the distant rumbling of the volcano that's about to blow, and as soon as I hear that, the explosion of a big eruption echoes across the Star Chamber.

18: MOON

He picks himself slowly up from the floor. Time, which once weighed down upon him as a crushing weight like the rock above him, is no longer. There is no forward, only around and around in the rhythm of wake and sleep, over and over in the endless dark.

At first he was confused. He couldn't remember how he got here. Then it came back to him. The frantic, fast movement through the woods, woods that seemed so dark then but which he now knows were positively bright compared to life here. Movement faster than his body could possibly do by itself, that much he remembers. But how? He racks his brain, finding nothing.

All of that must have been a dream. He remembers others like him, younger, but more like him than those who dwell here. That's how he knows his memory is but a dream. There are no others like him. Among the people of the dark, he is a monster, he is legend; he is the only one of his kind.

Since he was born into the real world, of darkness and rock, he's been haunted by the dreams of a place without the comforting roof of rock. His sleep has told him of a light so much brighter than the walls, a light high above that illumines the entire world, making the light of the walls here in the real world seem like mere shadows. Oh, what foolishness! How could such a thing be?

In his dreams, there are cycles of light and dark. When he wakes to reality, there is only dark and darker. Even the darkness is not dark, for the walls provide all the light that one could need. All that tracks the passage of time is the needs of his stomach. Fish can be found in the running waters, the only food he has ever eaten. Once he used the cycle of hunger and satisfaction to measure time. Nearly a thousand units had gone by, nine hundred and sixty-nine of them to be precise, before he realized what foolishness it was to count the days.

The world down here is all there is, that's the one thing he doesn't doubt. Why try to escape? Life above ground is but a dream.

19: SUN

Shaken, **Pedro** rises into a sitting position on the cave floor. My head hurts. I haven't had enough to drink. Oh man, I can't even remember where I am. What in the world just happened?

I look around. I'm in a fairly nondescript cave tunnel, just over my height high and wide enough for maybe two people to walk side by side. Blinking repeatedly, I try to figure out how I got here.

Then it hits me. I can see. There's no lantern, no electrical lighting, no bioluminescence. I can't be far from some source of daylight, even if it's high above.

And I'm not alone. No sign of Mabov or the other wolfmen or whatever they are, but less than twenty feet away from me, Brandon is slouching against the wall, looking half-awake. Kate's in the other direction, rubbing sleep from her eyes, and I have to say there's something incredibly alluring about the way she stretches and yawns. It's a sight I hope I'll see again. From the way she looks at me as she realizes I'm watching her wake up, I almost dare to hope she's glad I'm the first thing she sees.

"Holy fuck, what happened?", comes a voice from down the tunnel beyond Kate, away from the source of sunlight.

"I think we've found Chase", Kate says to me, standing up facing me and gesturing behind herself. I smirk and pull myself onto my feet.

Sure enough, Chase emerges from the darkness, followed closely by Jarri and Lily. They all look shell-shocked. Willy and Danny materialize behind them, and the five walk toward us. Brandon stands, and the eight of us walk toward the direction the light is coming from.

We emerge into a room with very high walls leading to a high ceiling. There are two places admitting light, one a narrow slit and the other a wider opening that seems to have more of a ledge blocking it off. Along the wall to our left, we can see a primitive wooden staircase leading upward, beams stuck in holes that must have been drilled into the rock. On the floor ahead of us lies a pile of tattered old clothes, mining tools, cooking pots and utensils, and coils of rope.

"Yeah," says Chase, "here we are again. I found this place during the night. Didn't realize it was this close to an exit. This is where I found the journal."

"What journal?", Kate and I ask in unison.

"This", he replies, holding out a tattered leather-bound book. "It's Edgar Allan Poe's."

"You serious?", I ask. This, I did not expect.

"His name's right here. I think we should read the last page."

As Chase starts to open the book to the final page, Jarri gets all of our attention by shouting "Whoa!", sounding almost involuntary. Everyone else turns to see that he is looking straight up.

"I think you can only see it from this spot", he says, not moving his head. Danny and Lily and I crowd around him and follow his gaze. A huge skull leers down at us from the ceiling.

"Cool rock formation", says Danny. "I wonder if that's natural or man-made?"

"The place of the skull", muses Lily. "Nice! The tomb's about to get empty."

I frown. "What do you mean, the tomb?"

"It *is* a tomb", says Jarri sadly.

Kate, joining us, realizes what he means. "Ricky and Trent?"

"They didn't make it."

"Poe did", says Chase. "He got out of here. Left this behind."

"Along with his rope?", asks Danny, who's now crouching by the pile of old equipment.

"Yeah. Here, look. 'I now understand the truth for which I may yet die. Deep in the heart of the cavern lies a bed of oil, the like of which I believe shall soon be usefull for many tasks beneficial to mankind. My visions were close to the truth. Darkness lies in the deeps, the darkness of a liquid that may light the world. Whoever knows of its source shall be a wealthy man. Alas, it is already known, and the men who hold claim to it will not suffer any other to share in their lucre. My friends and I should have been content with the upper parts of the cave. Instead we dug too greedily and too deep. I am the only one left who knows, unless Sarah indeed escaped with her life. Little time do I have left. I feel the foaming madness coming, what men of learning call hydrophobia. The bite has already unleashed foul humors into my blood. There is no time to find food or water or clothes my size. I ride swiftly for Washington to warn whomever I find there, though I fear my faculties of navigation are quite diminished. May the Lord have mercy on my poor soul."

Chase closes the book. "Not quite how I thought it would end. He never really says what the creatures he met down here were."

"He overshot Washington", Kate muses, "and ended up in Baltimore. Must have found a horse at some farmstead around here and ridden day and night. Well, we've shed some light on that mystery. Nobody ever knew what Poe died from after they found him in that gutter. Looks like it was rabies that did him in."

"Well, at least none of us have rabies. Nobody's been bitten by anything down here, right?"

Nobody answers me directly, but I'm hoping if anyone had they'd at least say something.

"Okay, we've got some rope, there's stairs here; Kate, will we be able to use this rope to climb up and out? You're the only one of us who's been in here on a rope before."

"We don't need any rope", says Danny suddenly.

"And what makes you say that?", I ask, rounding on him.

"Look", he says. "There's another tunnel out right here. See, there was this rock blocking the end, but when I rolled it away…"

We now see that Danny is standing in front of an opening big enough for any of us to crawl through. I walk up to it and look up. Sure enough, daylight at the other end. It's a straight passage, clearly man-made, going up at an angle to what must be the bottom of a valley, on the side of the hill opposite our campsite.

"Danny", I admit, "you're a lot smarter than most people think, aren't you?"

Only when all eight of us have crawled up to the surface and are out of the caves does he answer.

"Miranda was always an honors student, as you might have guessed. Everything somebody could achieve in high school, she did it. Her resume was loaded. Mission trips to Latin America and Africa, check. Some internship somewhere, many hours of service projects, extracurriculars, check, check, check. She had the grades, she had the recognition, she was going to go to an Ivy League school, and she was absolutely miserable. I could hear her through the wall between our bedrooms, sobbing into her pillow every single night for three or four years. The pressure was driving her insane.

"Our parents had no idea. They saw only the side she presented to the world. They never wondered why she always wore long sleeves. To hide the marks from where she kept cutting herself, you know. They couldn't see how the need to achieve had broken her. Then senior year came around, and she came back from fall break pregnant. I thought our parents were going to throw her out of the house. They tried to cover it up. Pressured her to have an abortion, even though they have bumper stickers on their cars that say 'Pro-Life'. She refused. Managed to conceal it the whole spring semester. Even at graduation, only a few of her friends knew. She just managed to wear the right clothes. Hoodies and baggy pants all the time. She gave the baby up for adoption that summer and went onward to college like nothing had ever happened. But now it was just [he names the primary big public school of one of the adjacent states], because she hadn't kept up the pace that last semester and her resume ended at October.

"I was still in elementary school, and it wasn't time for me to start achieving yet, but I knew what was coming if I got labeled as smart like she did. Of course I know that Israel's not in Europe, other than in international sports. I have to do that kind of thing to keep up the appearance. Maybe I made the wrong choice…but maybe not. Life is so much easier for me, with no expectations at all. My parents will be happy if I just graduate high school with a C average and go off to [he names the state school again]. What am I really missing out on? Only things I'm better off without."

He then shuts his mouth and does not open it until we're back at the campsite.

The tents are all shredded and lying in ruined heaps, people's duffel bags and backpacks similarly lying strewn around all over the place. Lily's sketchbook and colored pencils are the only things we can see that haven't been trashed, sitting inside a sealed zip-lock bag atop a pile of stuff. Some of the logs that we used as the fire ring have huge gashes in them that weren't there the last time I saw the place, which I realize must have been yesterday morning before Danny and I headed off to find help and instead found Sep dead.

"Oh good, the van's still here", says Jarri, walking toward it and opening the door. Nothing happens as he does; nobody jumps out and attacks him, the van doesn't blow up, and he doesn't even set off the car alarm.

Kate, facing away from the road into the trees, sniffs the air uneasily. She turns to me, a worried look in her eyes.

"What is it?"

"Something's out there. We're not in the clear yet."

"I think I can hotwire this", says Jarri, who hasn't heard Kate.

"Cows again", says Willy, whom we all ignore.

"Can you do it quickly?", Kate asks.

"Just give me a sec. Here, I'll open the sliding door so you guys can all get in. We're going to have to fit four in the back."

Kate looks positively panicked, though not at Jarri's words.

"We have to get out of here now!", she hisses, gesturing wildly at everyone to climb in.

Too much has happened for us to ignore her. Lily is in the backseat before Kate says another word, followed by Brandon and Willy, who double-buckle in the middle of the back bench. Danny slips in next to them. Kate takes shotgun as Chase slides into the captain's chair behind Jarri in the driver's seat. The engine sputters and coughs and suddenly flares to life, Jarri cheers, and I jump into the remaining seat.

"Get it in drive! Quick!", Kate yells to Jarri, who complies. He drives off as I'm still shutting the sliding door.

And because the vehicle isn't in park, the sliding door won't shut. It just goes "bawmp bawmp bawmp bawmp bawmp" and won't move. As we roll down the gravel road, the noise of heavy footfalls pounds right next to the van, a snarling growl coming from the air right next to me. Whatever it is, it's invisible and it's trying to attack us. I can feel its hot breath as it opens its invisible jaws for the strike.

Jarri jams on the brakes and throws the van into park. The creature, unseen but definitely real, doesn't have the ability to stop as quickly and sounds like it's tumbling in a heap, fifteen or twenty feet ahead of the van. I put some muscle into the door and get it shut just as the creature thuds into it from outside. Jarri puts the van back into drive and zooms off down the road toward the town of Whitmer, earning enough traffic violations to guarantee he never gets a license in this country but getting us away from the danger. We zip around bend after bend in the road and don't stop until we've pulled into the crowded parking lot of a fast-food restaurant in town.

20: JUDGMENT

DECEMBER 2007
Charleston, West Virginia

"David John Kretschak, you are found guilty of negligent manslaughter in the deaths of September Lenore Janney, Trent Nolan Jackson, Thomas Uriah Robert Kretschak, and Richard David Kretschak. Your sentencing will occur on January 7. This court is adjourned."

David Kretschak, only a few days ago the designated successor for the position of Headmaster of Berghall Academy to begin duties over the course of the spring semester, shakes his head in resignation. The board has informed him that if he is found guilty of any of the dozen charges he has been facing, he will be not only denied the position but also terminated from the school altogether. Three students are dead, including his own son, their bodies pulled out of a creek in remote West Virginia. A fellow teacher, his own brother at that, is still missing and has been declared legally dead due to the circumstances. For the school to survive, they tell him, he has to be cut loose.

He knows darn well that they didn't arrive at this decision by themselves.

"Idiot never should have interfered", mutters the portly man sitting in the courtroom balcony, so that only the people on either side of him can hear.

The woman sitting to his left debates whether she should say anything. Conscience versus career, she knows the choice is, and she makes the decision that will haunt her for years to come.

Ovenden says nothing at all about how Oake was far more guilty of interfering than Kretschak was. Her boss already decided how they will react to the fiasco, a few days ago, when they informed Kretschak that he would take the fall for what happened to his students.

"I'm not the person you should be blaming for this!", David

Kretschak screams at the judge, repeating what he's been saying for the last two days, knowing that he has been outmaneuvered and defeated. He glares defiantly up into the balcony, knowing that two of the government agents who threw him under the bus and the man who pulls their strings are sitting right there, watching to make sure he sees the inside of a jail cell and they don't.

As David is hauled from the courtroom, looking far more like one of the kids he's accustomed to disciplining than like his usual self, Ovenden blinks back a tear of rage. She doesn't dare say anything to Vrienstma. The chubby mining company CEO who really owns Ovenden's agency is sitting there right beside her, a smug grin on his face, the look of a man who *always* gets what he wants. The slightest hint of disagreement from the twenty-six-year-old desk clerk would make her cease to be a desk clerk. It would be Flandell who officially fired her, she knows this, but she also knows that the older woman sitting on the other side of Vrienstma is little more than the CEO's pawn.

"So what really happened to those kids?", Vrienstma asks, in a tone that suggests he almost cares.

Flandell shakes her head. "Does it really matter? They died. None of the others saw anything."

"That teacher, the brother, he's not really dead, is he?"

"No. We've still got him under surveillance. He's been in the caves for two months, living off of fish from the underground streams. If he ever finds his way out, he'll be so crazy nobody will believe him. Won't even know his own name."

"So just like that pesky geologist near…was it Spencer or Glenville?"

"Glenville. Yes, just like him."

"Thanks for taking care of him, by the way. Bastard was nearly on to us."

"Any time, Jay. Any time."

"Well, it'll probably be the last time it goes that far. My buddies and I picked up enough seats in Congress last year that it'll probably be legalized soon. That's going to change things, you know. Instead of keeping violations under cover, you and your people will be showing the EPA and whoever else wants to get in the way of progress that everything my company does is legal."

Flandell has known this day would come, but it hadn't really sunk in until now. It's going to be weird finishing up the last years of her career with a clean conscience after all the corruption she has enabled through her position. Those kids will never be able to tell anyone about what was really going on in the deepest parts of the mine, and if anyone believes them, there'll be no scandal to report because the laws will have changed and all they really saw was legal business as usual.

Assuming, that is, that any of the kids can even figure out what they saw. As people file out of the courthouse, Vrienstma has one last question for Flandell.

"How did you know they were inside in the first place?"

"Quite simple, Jay. A camera setup inside the big room where they started rappelling. Normally it's not running, but one of the kids threw a rock and woke up the system. As soon as it was live, we knew who was inside the cave. The rest, you already know."

Vrienstma nods. "Ah, yes, that makes sense. Well, anyways, Elaine, thanks for all the work that you do. This final judgment is one I can live with." He shakes her hand, then extends his to Ovenden and doesn't notice her reluctance. "And Callie, keep up the good work, someday you'll have her job."

The mining CEO walks away.

"*Caitlin*", Ovenden mutters under her breath, "he does that every fricking time."

She doesn't mention that having Flandell's job in thirty years is not an appealing prospect. Flandell doesn't need to know that.

They walk down the sidewalk and into a nondescript four-door vehicle with government plates. As Ovenden climbs in, another missing piece of the puzzle hits her.

"Okay, boss, explain this one to me if you please. How did Oake manage to blow up his own car?"

"Oh, he didn't. He got that other teacher, Stillman, into his trunk once the last kid was separated from her. What he was planning to do with her, I have no idea. He also took along more than a hundred times as much Ussher as he was supposed to. That stuff's very combustible. Don't think he's going to have carte blanche in the future, believe me. Carter Oake is going to see what life on a short leash is like."

"Yeah, but how…"

"She tried to escape by setting fire to the cloth seats. No way she could have known what that would do. Honestly, it's a miracle she got out with nothing more than a bad sunburn. I might have expected her and Oake both to be nothing but charcoal."

"What is Ussher, anyway?"

Flandell chuckles. "That, dearie, is classified. Suffice to say it's a psychoactive chemical. If Oake had stuck to the script, the kids would just have run around in the woods for a day or two on a serious acid trip and forget they even knew the cave existed."

"So when you said, keep them in the dark, you really just meant…"

"Of course! Nobody was supposed to get killed. Nobody would have if Kretschak hadn't been spying on them through the cameras in the vans and tried to take matters into his own hands."

"You know, the day this all started, I really thought you and Remstine meant we were going to kill those kids."

"Oh please. Casualties are supposed to be collateral damage from the system working in the most profitable way, not deliberate actions of ours. You've been reading too many conspiracy theories."

21: WORLD

OCTOBER 2007
Whitmer, West Virginia

Now that the adrenaline of the harrowing drive into town has worn off, **Pedro** is just bored of the interior of the police station. We've been in here for hours and hours while they question each of us. September's and Trent's parents have been notified by phone of their tragic losses, but Ricky's father is already here in West Virginia, here at the station with us. Something doesn't sit right with me.

As in, I can't shake the feeling that he already knew.

"Alright", says the deputy, facing the eight of us from the other side of the room with Ricky's father standing next to him, "we might as well get this over with in one go. It's pretty obvious what happened, once we take all the evidence into account. Mr. Kretschak here has testified that September Janney was a profoundly disturbed, unhappy young lady who must have harbored some nasty inner demons. She took her own life yesterday around noon using one of the spare ropes from the rock climbing gear. Since she didn't know how to tie a firm knot, her body fell from the tree that she used to hang herself just after she died from asphyxiation."

"That's bullshit." Yes, I dare say it to the deputy, Gannasas or whatever his name is. Sure, he's still tough at about thirty and built like a football player, but I've stood up to scarier people than him.

But it's Mr. Kretschak (seriously, I wonder for the hundredth time in three and a half years, how are we students supposed to distinguish him from his younger brother who was on the trip with us?) who snaps at me to shut up. Gannasas just keeps going.

"Richard Kretschak fell to his death from a sixty-foot cliff while running around under the influence of meth. The eight of you looking at me right now are lucky you didn't fall off too. What you little punks were thinking, messing around with that stuff...we get this shit so often. Schools have got to do a better job keeping kids away from drugs."

"Excuse me?" This time it's Kate. "What is it you're saying we did?"

Gannasas stares at her without blinking, as if he's not used to having his pronouncements questioned. "The eleven of you took advantage of the lack of adult supervision two evenings ago and found the meth lab at [he gives an address that means nothing to me, nor, to judge from my classmates' reactions, to any of them]. After entering a drug-induced state, you little brats ran around in the woods causing all kinds of havoc and mayhem. You crashed into a local farmer's cattle pasture and attacked his livestock, causing the animals to stampede, which in turn caused Trent Jackson to be trampled to death as the rest of you fled with no concern for his safety. Then there's the matter of the attack on the homeless man by two of you, Pedro Alvarez and Daniel Stillman. Since your victim has declined to press charges, you're off the hook for that."

I have no idea what he's talking about.

"The eight of you then spun a ridiculous story to me about wandering into a cave and getting lost. That kind of thing really does happen to people sometimes. Shame on you for using that as your excuse. If I or another of my colleagues had got lost underground looking for you, you'd *really* be in trouble."

Just then, there's a commotion down the hallway. We all look just in time to see Miss Stillman being led into the room in handcuffs by a female officer.

"We had an anonymous eyewitness report that five of you here, and that's Kathryn Bauer, William Cunningham, Jerry Kug..."

"*Yahr*-ree."

"Okay, Yahr-ree Kugman-Tor...oh forget it, Chase Creighton, and Brandon Parsons, were seen breaking into a vehicle parked at a popular hiking trailhead and possibly stealing items. Again, you're off the hook there because she [he gestures to Miss Stillman] set fire to the vehicle and destroyed it. I know one of you came up with this hysterical report of a volcano erupting...that must have been the explosion when the gas tank blew up."

"But, out of the goodness of his heart, my boss has decided to let you off with a warning. It will be up to your school to decide what punishment you deserve. We've arranged for you all to get on a school bus and be driven back to Cincinnati. Your effects that could be recovered from the campsite – and there's not much left after all the ruckus you caused – will be waiting for you in that room over there. Go on, get a move on."

I'm the last to file out of the room, and I notice what none of the others do except for Kate, just ahead of me. Mr. Kretschak reaches his hand out to shake hands with Deputy Gannasas, and instead Gannasas whips out a pair of handcuffs and slaps them on the calculus teacher's wrist.

Kate and I freeze in the doorway, dying of curiosity.

"David Kretschak, I'm placing you under arrest for contributing to the delinquency of a minor. Eleven of them, actually. You have the right to remain silent."

"What on earth is this?" Mr. Kretschak isn't using his right.

"I have it right here," says Gannasas, "right here on your own statement that you made to one of my colleagues. You took specific actions to ensure that this trip would be a disaster and the young people on it would get involved with drugs. You went so far as to sign up a young man with a lengthy track record of drug problems for the trip at the last minute, just to guarantee…oh you know what, it's going to be worse for you than delinquency of a minor. Your actions led to at least three deaths and possibly four."

"You did *what?*", Kate and I can hear Miss Stillman shout at Mr. Kretschak. She spits in his face before the cop holding her handcuffs hustles her away. Then we too are hustled down the hall.

*****

"You're disqualified from being valedictorian. Such a shame, Alvarez. You really had a shot at it."

I hang my head, but not necessarily in shame, at Mr. Ekdahl's words. The elderly headmaster looks ten years older than he did a few weeks ago. I can't be angry with him for taking this chance away from me; all I can feel at the moment is pity for what a sad situation he's been put in so close to the end of his career.

It's fine. I don't need to be valedictorian to live a fulfilling life. But I'm not leaving the room until I see what other consequences are meted out. Lily's fine, that much I've seen, but they're still putting her on probation for some reason, just like they did to me before making the decision to remove me from the valedictorian list. I suspect everyone else will share this fate.

Danny's brought in, and sure enough, probation it is. Same for Jarri and Willy. Brandon protests, when it's his turn, that he did nothing, but Mr. Ekdahl replies that the police received a report of him violently shoving Trent just half an hour or so before Trent was trampled by cows.

"Is that true?", I whisper to Kate.

"Well, technically yes", she sighs.

Then she says something I can't believe I'm hearing.

"Pedro, do you love me?"

I gulp, but I nod. I can't make myself say a word.

Pretending that didn't just happen, we watch as Chase is brought up next.

"Chase Creighton. What the dickens are we supposed to do with you? You have a record from your previous school in Paducah of drug possession, vandalism, public urination…and now we have Mr. Kretschak's testimony that you physically attacked his son during the first night of the trip. Richard is dead now. Do you understand that in a court of law, it could look like you had something to do with his death?"

"I had nothing to do with that."

"Do you love me, Pedro?", Kate asks again, whispering even more quietly. Again, I nod, listening to Mr. Ekdahl.

"I believe you, Chase, but we have to do what we have to do. Consider yourself expelled from Berghall Academy. Since Trent is dead too now, the Jacksons have said you do not belong under their roof anymore. You'll need to return home and your parents can figure out the best course of action."

I probably don't need to describe Chase's reaction in much detail.

"I'm guessing Miranda probably loses her job over this?", Kate says to me.

"Yeah, she already has. They just haven't told the student body yet."

"So not fair."

I'm about to agree when Kate herself is called to the stand. Surely this will just be a formality like with me or Lily.

"Kathryn Bauer. My goodness. What are we to do...we have the testimony of young Mr. Cunningham that you repeatedly struck him, threatened him with physical violence, attacked his religious beliefs, and used abusive language toward him on several occasions. This, combined with your lengthy disciplinary record of bringing weapons onto school property, makes me very concerned.

"Your conduct has been thoroughly unladylike and indeed aggressive. Such behavior cannot be tolerated at Berghall. We are, after all, a Christian school. It's up to us to set the standard that the rest of the world lives by."

My sympathy for poor old Mr. Ekdahl goes out the window. I get up and walk over to Kate's side. She will not face this alone.

She looks me in the eye. It's only now that I realize just how beautiful her eyes are.

"Pedro," she says out loud, "do you love me?"

"Yes," I finally dare to say, "I love you, Kate."

"Then do exactly as I say."

Mr. Ekdahl clears his throat and glares at her. "Have you nothing to say in your defense, Miss Bauer?"

Kate glares back at him. "Mr. Ekdahl, I always thought you were better than this. I'm sorry that I was so wrong about you."

"Careful, young lady. You are only increasing the discipline that must be applied for the sake of correction."

"No. I'm not getting one more detention from this school."

Then Kate does something that surprises even me. She turns, throws her arms around me, and kisses me smack on the lips. Not a quick peck, either. Her lips are pulsing, her tongue's getting in on the action…um, yeah. Wow. There's nothing I can say. Even if I had my mouth free. Because we weren't violating Berghall's rule against public displays of affection already, Kate then grabs my hand and pulls it up into her shirt. I wouldn't have tried that anytime soon. Welp, I have now had my hand cupped around a bare breast. Figures she doesn't wear a bra. I am *so* glad she's older than me and was eighteen before I was. I pull my hand back out of her shirt as quickly as I can. Meanwhile, she's using hers to flip the bird at Mr. Ekdahl.

"You have *nothing* you can use against me, Mr. Ekdahl, because I've already withdrawn from Berghall. I figured something like this might happen ever since I figured out that Willy was planning to try to get Mr. Kretschak in trouble. Thomas, I mean. So, I stopped by the registrar this morning and made it official. I am *not* a student at your school anymore, so you know what?"

She kisses her hand and spanks herself with it, pointing her butt toward Mr. Ekdahl and the school board.

"Okay then", she says to me, grabbing the front of my shirt with both of her hands and leaning in one more time, "you know how to get hold of me, right?" I nod, she winks, and just like that she's gone from the room.

Mr. Ekdahl looks speechless. Actually, he *is* speechless.

"Well, that's a new one", says one of the parents on the board. "At least that's the end of…"

Kate sticks her head back into the room, raising her fists to the sky triumphantly.

"Hey, your God got nailed to a cross. Mine carries a hammer. Any questions? HAIL THOR!"

Now I can't help it. I'm doubled over laughing as Kate, I imagine, beats a hasty retreat from the building, never to return.

I know I'm going to worry a lot in the next few months about whether I'm ever going to see her again. It's a big world out there, easy for people to get separated in. But somehow, I know I will. I just hope the deck hasn't been shuffled too much between now and then.

EPILOGUE: FOOL

The cycle begins anew.

I finish telling my story and grow silent. Mr. Boval just sits there and nods, deep in thought. Eventually he stands and I do the same. It's late into the evening, and some of the kids on this trip are going to bed already. I'm glad Willy's among them. That little shit is the reason I haven't seen Kate in almost five months. I still don't even know if she's in Cincinnati anymore, although I suspect not. I like to think the reason I'm not hearing from her is that she's currently off on some lengthy backpacking trip with no electronics. If the reason is anything else, I'm going to be haunted forever by the thought of what might have been.

"Yes, you will", says Boval at last.

I don't pretend to not know what he means. Boval, I think, can read minds.

"How do you know?", I ask, hoping he's right.

"I'm older than I look. I've seen this kind of thing happen before, many times. When there's a spark to begin with, the one who goes wandering away always comes back. Give her another month. You will see her again…plenty of her."

I don't let myself think about ways to interpret that.

"In fact," Mr. Boval continues, "I'd like to meet her. Find out what her summer plans are. If she's free for the beginning of July, I've got a project that I want to recruit the two of you for, not far from here.

"Montenegro is home to the Mediterranean's only fjord, the Bay of Kotor, about a three-hour drive southeast of here. Come summertime, there's going to be an archaeological dig at a Stone Age settlement on the north shore, in one of the few areas that hasn't been disturbed in all this time. I'm leading the dig for two weeks and would very much like to have you and Kate be among my assistants."

"Why us?"

"You've looked into the Heart of the Raven and lived to tell the tale."

"I wouldn't place much stake in that. We never even figured out what the Heart of the Raven meant. Is it the oil deposits in the deepest parts of the caves? This mining company has started working to extract it in the past month, using a method that Congress just signed a law making legal. What it does to the environment...ugh. Anyway, what the heck does it mean that we looked into a deep hidden oil well and returned? How can that be a meaningful statement?"

Boval frowned. "Perhaps you are indeed the Fool. You shortchange the value of a rare experience you've had. I do not think you are a foolish person, though. Give it time. You've seen much in your life. So has she. But what I want your expertise for is, well, the cave creatures. It sounds like you stumbled upon a colony of Psoglav. Dog-headed men of Serbian and Montenegrin myth. These days, they live underground, but..."

"We didn't meet any dog-headed men. They were hallucinations. We got drugged by a government goon who splashed us with huge quantities of hallucinogens and tried to make it look like we found a meth lab. That's all that happened. There were never any caves, do you understand that?"

"I understand that that's what they told you. And you know damn well that it's a bunch of lies. The version you told me makes a better story, and not just because it's more entertaining. It's truer. When you live as long as I have, you recognize patterns in the human experience. You see the ways that people live and act, and you know how to call bullshit when someone makes a claim that doesn't fit with the card deck of human behavior patterns."

"So you believe me?"

"Yes. And I need you and Kate because the excavation is of a colony of Psoglav from way back before they went underground."

To be continued: look for The Letterstorm in early 2017

BIBLIOGRAPHY, WORKS INSPIRED BY, AND SUGGESTIONS FOR FURTHER READING
In no particular order:

Edgar Allan Poe, complete works, especially *The Narrative of Arthur Gordon Pym* and *Murders in the Rue Morgue*

Dante Alighieri, *Divine Comedy*

J.R.R. Tolkien, *The Hobbit*

Herman Melville, *Moby Dick*

Carl Jung, *The Red Book*

Charlotte Bronte, *Jane Eyre*

Joseph Conrad, *Heart of Darkness*

C.S. Lewis, *Chronicles of Narnia*, esp. *The Silver Chair*

Yann Martel, *Life of Pi*

F. Scott Fitzgerald, *The Diamond as Big as the Ritz*

Karen Hamaker-Zondag, *Tarot as a Way of Life*

Jean Auel, *Earth's Children* series

Cormac McCarthy, *The Road*

Albert Sanchez Pinol, *Pandora in the Congo*

Barbara Brown Taylor, *Learning to Walk in the Dark*

Gil Stafford, *Pilgrimage as a Way of Life*, forthcoming

S.D. Gloria, *Tamyth* trilogy

And of course: Michael Piers, *Golden Plague*. I had to do it.

ACKNOWLEDGMENTS

Besides those to whom the book is dedicated, I wish to thank those who made this book possible. My parents, Paul and Marie, for sustaining me through a very challenging time. Extended family – Elizabeth, Fred, Ann, Leah, Klaus, C.K., and Hielkje – for helping *Golden Plague* to see the light of day. Friends close to home – Gil, Cathy, Blair, Philip, Thad – who kept me in the light so this could get finished. Rawleigh, my super-awesome roommate, for making my house a home again and being one of the first to place his seal of approval on this manuscript. The others who gave me their time to read it and let me know it was ready – Cynthia, Steven, Candace, Karin, Rebecca, another Michael P who made possible the Balkan travels that inspired both *Golden Plague* and this book, and most of all Suzanne, the co-author of my *next* next book and of many more projects to come.

ABOUT MICHAEL PIERS

Michael Piers ("Mikh-HILE Pierce") is a twenty-first-century shaman, druid, and education theorist. His previous book, *Golden Plague*, combines the ancient plot of Jason and the Argonauts with a gripping modern quest to find a vanished missile and prevent the Golden Fleece from becoming the weapon that destroys a civilization. He is also the author of a short play relating the long-term experience of a survivor of the 1995 Siege of Sarajevo, the research for which inspired a significant element of *Golden Plague*. Michael has previously lived in the Midwest and inland East Coast, as well as Budapest and Athens, but now makes his home in Arizona with his two cats, the energetic Orca and the profoundly spiritual Raven.

Made in the USA
Columbia, SC
04 December 2017